Wycliffe and the Cycle of Death

By W. J. Burley

W. J. BURLEY

Wycliffe and the Cycle of Death

A CRIME CLUB BOOK
DOUBLEDAY
New York London Toronto Sydney Auckland

A CRIME CLUB BOOK
PUBLISHED BY DOUBLEDAY
a division of
Bantam Doubleday Dell Publishing Group, Inc.
666 Fifth Avenue, New York, New York 10103

DOUBLEDAY and the portrayal of a man
with a gun are trademarks of
Doubleday, a division of Bantam Doubleday Dell
Publishing Group, Inc.

This story is set in Penzance and its immediate neighbourhood but I have changed
the topography a little to reduce any risk that readers may see accidental
resemblances to actual living persons in the characters portrayed.
All the characters and events in this book are imaginary.

Library of Congress Cataloging-in-Publication Data
Burley, W. J. (William John)
Wycliffe and the cycle of death / W. J. Burley.
p.   cm.
"A Crime Club book."
I. Title.
PR6052.U647W875   1990   90-23331
823'.914—dc20   CIP

ISBN 0-385-41800-0
Copyright © 1990 by W. J. Burley

Wycliffe and the Cycle of Death

CHAPTER ONE

Saturday

Charles Wycliffe, detective chief superintendent, and Matthew Glynn, bookseller and district councillor, were spending their Saturday eighty miles apart with no idea that their paths would cross; in fact, in ignorance of each other's existence.

Wycliffe had a free weekend and intended to enjoy it at home with his wife in their house on the Tamar estuary. Matthew Glynn expected to spend most of his day in the shop: Glynn's of Penzance, one of the most prestigious bookshops in the county.

It was a remarkably warm April morning and the Wycliffes ate their breakfast toast and drank their coffee out-of-doors on the paved terrace in front of the house. A blackbird asserted its territorial claims from a maple tree; in the pond, three or four goldfish chased a gravid female, churning the water into turmoil; and the Wycliffe cat, pretending that food did not come in tins, stalked invisible mice in the herbaceous border.

At about the same time, Matthew Glynn was in the bathroom, shaving; he had not taken to electric razors, preferring the ritual of soaping his face and cleaving a path through to the smooth skin in a minimum number of strokes. But this was becoming more of a challenge as the furrows deepened year by year. Now when he looked in the mirror he saw his father's face as he most clearly remembered it, lean and gaunt, grey and lined—the Glynn face.

But there was a difference: he carried the mark. He could not have described the mark or explained exactly what he meant, but it was there and sometimes he wondered why others could not see it.

He was fifty-two; not yet old, but over the hill, definitely.

Wycliffe was not brooding upon his age but counting his blessings from a comfortable cane chair. The rhododendrons and azaleas were coming into their own, the magnolias and camellias were at their best, and through a screen of trees at the bottom of the garden he could glimpse the shining waters of the estuary. Altogether, at that moment, there was little to remind him that all is vanity under the sun.

He settled more comfortably in his chair. If he had been a cat he would have purred.

Helen poured a second cup of coffee. "It's going to be a good weekend!"

Matthew Glynn, back in his bedroom, knotted his tie and put on the woolly cardigan he wore in the shop. His father had worn a tailor-made three-piece, summer and winter, and a white shirt with gold cuff-links. "Mr. Glynn is always immaculate," the women used to say.

Matthew combed the remnants of his hair. In the mirror, behind his own image, he could see his bed—an old-fashioned and massive double bed, made up for one. "I'm a lonely man," he told himself.

A morning for reflections.

Outside the sun was shining and from the window of his bedroom Matthew could see Mount's Bay, level and serene. Once he had imagined that middle age might be like that, a plateau, a period of equipoise before the final descent. Instead he found himself, like Alice's Red Queen, having to run faster and faster to stay where he was.

The Red Queen reminded him of chess, chess reminded him of Ronnie Swayne, and Ronnie Swayne reminded him of money.

A bell rang somewhere in the house and Wycliffe said: "The postman."

Helen got up from her chair. "I'll go."

She was soon back with a little sheaf of letters and a wad of junk mail by courtesy of reluctant trees.

An air mail envelope received priority notice. "It's from David" —their son, who was working in Kenya. Helen slit open the envelope with a buttery knife, spread the pages, and scanned her son's scrawling script. She was excited. "They're coming home! In July . . ."

"For good?"

"Two months, then they expect to go back to Nairobi on a new contract."

"They'll be pleased about that."

"Jonathan has two teeth . . ."

Matthew Glynn went downstairs. He could hear his son's voice coming from the dining-room. As he pushed open the door it would cease as though a switch had been thrown.

His son, Gerald, and his elder daughter, Gina, were already at table. They acknowledged him as he sat down. Gerald was twenty-seven, a couple of years older than Gina. Gina fished in the muesli packet for extra raisins; Gerald cut a sausage in two, speared one portion on his fork, then popped it in his mouth followed by a piece of toast. Matthew poured himself a cup of coffee.

The Glynn dining-room faced the yard, which caught the morning sun, but the room itself was gloomy: faded wallpaper, brown-painted woodwork, dark oak furniture and drab fabrics. Cobwebs hid in the corners of the dusty cornice.

For the sake of saying something Matthew asked: "Where's Barry?" Barry was his son-in-law, Gina's husband.

"Jogging—it's Saturday."

An accountant, Barry did not work on Saturdays.

Gerald cleared his mouth of food and looked at his father, about to speak. Matthew, knowing what was coming, forestalled him: "You said your piece yesterday, Gerald. Give it a rest."

Father and son, out of the same mould, confronted one another. Gerald dropped his gaze and said nothing.

Sara, Matthew's sister, came in from the kitchen wearing the sombre grey overall she used for work. Every inch a Glynn, Sara was dark, big boned, and gaunt; her clothes hung from her shoulders as though from a coat-hanger. She brought with her a fresh supply of toast and a boiled egg.

"Oh, you're down, Matthew. Do you want an egg?"

"No—no, thank you." Matthew buttered some toast. He watched his sister eating, her every movement was precise and economical; she ate without pleasure, as though each mouthful

was a self-inflicted penance. She was three or four years younger
than he and though they had been brought up together, living in
the same house, they had never had any real contact. Yet if ever
anyone saw and recognized the mark, it would be Sara.

Years ago, when his wife left, Sara had taken over the running
of the house and the bringing up of his children. His parents were
alive then but living the life of a retired couple. Nobody had asked
Sara to step into the gap, the matter was never discussed. Sara was
there, and she did what was necessary without apparent enthusiasm or resentment.

Matthew sighed and three pairs of eyes turned on him.

The long-case clock cleared its throat in preparation for striking. Matthew got up and switched on the radio which stood on
the sideboard. The "pips" coincided with the first strokes of the
clock and were echoed by the church clock close by. The News.

Wycliffe went into the house through the French window to
switch on the News and stayed to listen to the usual litany of
disaster, wars, famine, and crime.

"And now a summary of the weather: a complex area of low
pressure is expected to reach the extreme south-west by early evening, bringing with it squally showers, mist, and drizzle . . ."

He refused to be bludgeoned out of his euphoria and rejoined
Helen on the terrace. "I think I'll cut the grass."

"It's still wet, we've had a heavy dew; you'll have to wait for it to
dry out."

He stood, hands thrust into his trouser pockets, surveying the
garden.

Helen said: "That shirt, Charles! It's filthy; you can't be seen in
that."

"I don't intend to be seen." But the pristine brightness of the
day was already tarnished.

Matthew Glynn switched off the radio and returned to his
place; he poured himself another cup of coffee. He saw Gerald and
Gina exchange glances; something had passed between them: a
signal? Recently he had become convinced that there was something going on behind his back; he read disturbing meanings into
the looks they exchanged; even into their silences. Was it his imag-
ination?

Christine, his younger daughter came in, still in her dressing gown, her eyes puffed with sleep. She looked very young and vulnerable. Christine was a student nurse in the local hospital and this was her free weekend.

"Isn't there any Shredded Wheat?" No one answered and she stood for a moment, looking over the table. She met her father's eyes. "Anyway, I don't think I'll bother with breakfast."

Sometimes he thought that what went on around him might be entirely comprehensible if only he could crack the code.

He got up from his chair. "I shall be in the shop."

The shop, which adjoined the house, was reached by a communicating door on the ground floor. Glynn & Son. New, Second-hand, and Rare Books. Established 1886. It was a large shop, double fronted, with bays after a fashion that was current in bookshops before shop-lifting became a national sport. Second-hand and rare books were housed on the floor above.

Matthew went to the switchboard and lights flicked on in the bays, then he made his way to the back of the shop where there were two offices, his own, and a smaller one for his typist. His office had a window and a door to the sunlit backyard which it shared with the house.

Gerald came in, tight lipped, and held out his hand for the keys to open up. Gerald was responsible for the new book trade; Gina would be upstairs with the second-hand and rare books. A family concern. Paula James, his typist, arrived by the back door.

"Good morning, Mr. Glynn!"

"Good morning, Paula."

Paula was eighteen and plump; addicted to short, tight skirts and plunging necklines. She disappeared into the toilet.

A day like any other.

Matthew dictated two or three letters about delayed orders and queried accounts; a local author came in, trying to arrange a signing session for his new book but anxious to have it understood that he was conferring a favour.

At half-past ten Paula made coffee.

Hours of idleness vanish like salt in water and by lunchtime Wycliffe had done nothing but moon about the garden, digging out the odd weed. At half-past twelve they had lunch on the terrace and the sun still shone. Afterwards he read the newspaper and dozed in his chair. Helen looked at him with affection.

That Saturday afternoon, trade at the bookshop was brisk and Matthew Glynn found himself serving in the shop for most of it. At five-thirty they closed, cashed up, and Gerald went to put the takings in the night safe at the bank.

At six-thirty they sat down to their evening meal, the whole family. For some reason there was more talk than usual. Barry, Matthew's son-in-law, was musical and was off to a choir practice; Christine was going to an amateur dramatics thing at St. John's Hall; Gerald was playing in a snooker tournament in St. Ives . . . They talked to each other, even involving Sara, but not to him. When the meal was over he stood up, looked around at his family, and said: "I think I shall go over to Ronnie Swayne's for an hour or two." For some odd reason it seemed that he was making a declaration.

Later they would say that this was the last time any of them had seen him alive.

The Wycliffes had their evening meal at a table by the window, enjoying the misty twilight, watching the colours fade and the emergence of twinkling lights in the estuary.

"Anything on television?"

"No."

"Do you feel like a walk to the village?"

So they walked to the village and had a drink in the pub where the landlord collected ships in bottles and there was a Saturday-night sing-along. Walking home, they could see the distant lights of the city flaring in the night sky.

Wycliffe said: "Tomorrow I'll do something."

Matthew Glynn held his remaining bishop poised and muttered under his breath: "Bishop to R5."

Ronnie Swayne raised his head in order to see the board through his half-glasses, then the little freckled hand swooped. "Rook to Kt7."

When a game was approaching its climax the two were in the habit of announcing their moves as though to lend them increased significance, and because they were both past middle age they used the old notation.

Glynn pondered, kneading his rather prominent nose between finger and thumb. "Knight to R4."

"Queen takes pawn."

"Queen takes queen."

With a thin smile Swayne administered the *coup de grâce.* "Bishop takes queen."

Glynn sat back, meditative and rueful. "No point in playing it out. Wasn't it Bardelebden, in a similar plight, who put on his hat and walked quietly home?"

Swayne chuckled. "That's the story."

They were in Ronnie Swayne's sitting-room. A heavily shaded standard lamp illuminated a small area around the fireplace: the mantelpiece with its marble clock and matching vases, the chessboard on a low table, the two armchairs . . . On one arm of Swayne's chair a huge tabby cat lay couchant, paws and tail tucked in. The pool of light failed to reach most of the room but, with the curtains undrawn, a streetlamp cast crooked shadows on the ceiling.

Glynn brooded on the chessboard and the evidence of his defeat. The marble clock chimed and struck nine.

Swayne, a neighbour of the Glynns, lived over his tiny shop where he traded in stamps, coins, and medals. Over the years he had carved out for himself a notable place in the strange world of dealers and collectors. He was a fierce-looking little man with strands of red hair combed across the freckled desert of his skull.

"Don't take it to heart, Matt; we all have our off-days."

Glynn grimaced. "I don't mind being beaten but I don't like being crucified."

"Then set 'em up again and have your revenge; the night is young."

"No, Ronnie, I'd like to but not tonight. I've work to do in the office. I'll chalk this one up to experience." Glynn was replacing the ivory chessmen in their box where each had its velvet-lined recess.

Swayne picked up a whisky bottle from the floor by his chair. "All right, if you won't stay, just a small one before you go." He poured a generous tot and passed over the glass followed by the water jug. "You were off form tonight, Matt, and no wonder—other things on your mind."

Glynn sipped his whisky. "You can say that again!" He went on, very tentative now: "I don't suppose you've any news for me yet?"

Swayne spread his hands, his manner apologetic. "It's early days, Matt, but my contact tells me he's been in touch with an interested party."

"Any figure mentioned?"

A reluctant smile. "You know already we shan't be talking about value at auction or anything like it. At this stage $50,000 US has been mentioned but that's only a basis for bargaining."

Glynn did some mental arithmetic. "About £31,000; perhaps a quarter of their true value."

Swayne stiffened. "True value! From your experience in the rare book trade, Matt, you must know there's no such thing. It's the same in my business, value depends on the market you sell in."

Glynn was embarrassed. "Yes, yes of course! I'm not being ungrateful, Ronnie, just working things out."

Swayne leaned forward in his chair. "Look, Matt, I shall be in London next week and I'll have a word—see if I can't stir up a bit of competition."

Glynn was doubtful. "I can't afford to risk starting any gossip."

"Neither can I, so don't worry."

Glynn finished his whisky and stood up. "You're being very good about this, Ron, and I shan't forget it."

"Nonsense!"

The clock chimed the half-hour as Glynn was leaving. Swayne went with him and the cat padded after them down the stairs and out into the yard.

Glynn laughed. "Clarence, off on his nightly prowl—he comes in to see me sometimes . . . Well, good night, Ronnie, and thanks."

He walked the few steps up the back lane to his own yard and entered by the plank door. He was about to shoot the bolt but changed his mind and left it unsecured. The wind was blowing in gusts bringing flurries of rain, but overhead the cloud was still broken.

In the drawing-room Gina had fallen asleep watching a film on television. Images flickered across the screen and a gas fire burned on the hearth but there was no other light. The drawing-room was in the front of the house, the window overlooking the street, where traffic was sporadic.

The front door opened and closed and a moment or two later her sister, Christine, came in looking slightly flushed; raindrops glistened on the collar of her anorak and in her hair.

Gina opened her eyes. "Hullo! Is it raining?"

"Showers."

Gina yawned. "I must have dropped off. What time is it?"

"Half-past ten. I'm going to make a hot drink. Would you like anything?"

"I wouldn't mind a cup of Horlicks or cocoa or something— whatever you're making. Be a dear! Switch off the TV and put the lights on. I'm not watching whatever it is."

"Is everybody else out?"

"Aunt Sara's up in her room, Gerald and Barry are still out, and Father is next door playing chess with Ronnie Swayne."

The sisters had the dark hair and eyes of the Glynns but their pale, oval faces with a tendency to freckles must have come from their absent mother or they were the outcome of a genetic com-promise. Gina was well covered; Christine, an inch or two taller, had the slim, rather bony physique of the Glynns.

Christine took off her anorak and went through to the kitchen. A few minutes later she was back with a tray: milky drinks and biscuits.

"Father must be in his office, I could see the light from the kitchen."

"Where did you go this evening?"

"I told you; the amateur dramatics thing at St. John's Hall."

"Oh yes, *A Doll's House.* Any good?"

"I thought so: Stella Gibbs as Nora was really good. Didn't you do Ibsen for your special paper in Finals?"

"For my sins."

Christine was pensive. "Tonight I thought I might have got some idea of why Mother walked out on us."

"Because Father was another Helmer and Mother, another Nora—is that it?" Gina was derisive.

Christine flushed. "All right! I don't remember Mother; I just thought, knowing Father, it could have been like that."

Gina took a second biscuit, dunked it in her drink, and avoided the implied question. "One thing's certain, Ibsen understood women and he's one of the few playwrights who did. Shakespeare didn't—all that stuff with the Lear sisters. And Desdemona! Every time I think of that woman I want to spit!"

Christine chuckled. "I wish I'd tried your line on old Ellis when I was at school."

"You'd have ended up with a delta. Who did you go with— David?"

"Yes." Defensive.

"So it's getting serious. Father won't be keen on you getting mixed up with Uncle Maurice and David with things as they are."

Christine fiddled with her bracelet then, abruptly, she looked up: "Gina, I'm not going on with nursing."

Her sister paused in the act of nibbling a biscuit. "Not going on? What the hell are you talking about?"

"I'm going in with them at the pottery; they need more help, I've enjoyed working there in my off-time, and they say I've got the makings of a potter . . ."

The words which had been tumbling out suddenly dried up.

"And?"

"Well, it's different from here—the atmosphere. I mean, we always seem so tense and nobody . . ."

"Nobody what?"

"I don't know."

"So when are you planning to make this change? I suppose you'll give yourself time to think, time to talk it over at the hospital and with Father?"

She became sullen. "I've done all the thinking and talking I intend to do and I've handed in my notice at the hospital. As a matter of fact it expired yesterday."

Gina was shaken. "God! Father will have a stroke! Are you going to marry David?"

"Perhaps. I shall be living there anyway."

"You do realize that Father and Uncle Maurice may go to law over Trebyan?"

Christine's eyes had reddened. "I can't help it, Gina. I can't see it Father's way. I'm on their side—it would be criminal to build houses out there. With Father it's money—always money!"

Gina reached out to put her mug on the tray. "You can't get far without it but I don't suppose what I say will make any difference. What is it about David that gets you? Is it sex?"

"No, it damn well isn't!" Christine paused. "Well, sex comes into it, but it isn't everything, not even the main thing. Dave believes in something—a way of life that doesn't destroy things or people and he's prepared to work for it. Surely you can see that there must be people who are ready to . . . to . . ."

"Stand up and be counted?"

"You're laughing at me!"

Gina shook her head. "No. I'm not laughing at you, Chris, not really. Perhaps I'm a tiny bit envious."

They heard the front door open.

"There's Barry now."

Barry came in and stood, blinking in the light, aware that once more he had blundered into a situation.

Barry Morse was fair and too delicately made so that his good looks were almost feminine. He was shortsighted and he wore gold-rimmed spectacles which enlarged his dark blue eyes in a way that could be disquieting.

"Is Gerald in?"

"Not yet."

Barry looked at Christine, then at his wife. "Yes, well . . . I think I'll go straight up."

"Don't you want anything?"

He hesitated, pondering the question. "No, I don't think so, thank you." He turned to Christine: "I'll say good-night, then." At the door, he looked back at his wife. "See you later."

Suddenly it seemed to Christine very odd that in a little while her sister would be getting into bed with this man.

Gina picked up the tray. There was a commotion at the front door, the door slammed, and there were heavy footsteps in the passage.

"Gerald."

Gerald was big boned and lean like his father, but nurturing an embryonic beer belly. His dark hair was wet and there were raindrops on his cheeks.

"The old man locked me out! I put the car away and tried to come in by the back door as usual but he's slipped the bloody bolt. I had to walk round the block and it's raining. I'm bloody wet!"

Gina said: "Poor you, but I don't suppose it will be fatal."

"He did it on bloody purpose! Spite, because I spoke my mind yesterday."

"You upset him."

"It's time somebody did; if we go on as we're going we shall end up in queer street."

Sara crossed the yard, running blindly. By the kitchen door she stopped, holding on to the door latch to steady herself. Her heart was racing and she had difficulty in breathing. She made a determined effort to take slow, deep breaths. It made her feel giddy at first and she was afraid she might faint, but after a little while she began to feel better.

She tried to see into the kitchen through a slit in the curtains; the light was on but there was no one there. With great care she opened the kitchen door, stopping short of the position where she knew it would squeak. A moment later she was inside; a few steps and she had reached the passage. The light was on there also but that was usual. She could hear voices coming from the sitting-room—Gerald's and Gina's.

Six paces to the stairs. They were carpeted but they creaked. She reached the landing, trembling but immensely relieved. At that moment someone flushed the lavatory at the end of the corridor and in panic she ran the few steps to the door of her room and went in, shutting and locking the door behind her regardless of noise.

She was in her sitting-room. For a long time she stood leaning against the door in the dark. Slowly her heart and her breathing returned to something like normal but the trembling had turned to shivering. She was cold. She switched on a light and lit the gas fire; she huddled in an armchair, pulling her wet raincoat about her, then she kicked off her shoes and held her stockinged feet to the warmth. She tried to think but her brain was numb. Then she noticed her shoes lying on the hearthrug and snatched them up. She examined them minutely, uppers, soles, and heels before dropping them once more on the floor.

CHAPTER TWO

Sunday morning

It was shortly before seven on Sunday morning when Wycliffe first heard of Matthew Glynn. He was still in bed when the call came through from the duty officer at CID headquarters.

"Sorry to disturb you, sir, so early on a Sunday morning, but we have a report of a homicide: Matthew Glynn, a bookseller, fiftyish, with a shop and house in Lady Street, Penzance, found dead in his office by his sister at 0605 this morning . . . The local DI says it looks as though he was strangled. This message timed at 0658 . . ."

Sunday. Usually rousing policemen or anybody else to a sense of urgency on a Sunday is like trying to stir cold treacle. Somebody must have done pretty well.

"All right; leave it with me."

Helen raised herself on her elbow. "You have to go out?"

"Penzance."

She put her feet over the side of the bed, reaching for her dressing gown. "I'll make some coffee."

He telephoned John Scales, his deputy. "I want a team, John: Kersey in charge, Shaw, Lucy Lane if she's available . . . I don't want an army; say three DCs in the first instance and see where we go from there . . . I'm driving down . . ."

Matthew Glynn, bookseller of Lady Street, Penzance; fiftyish . . . . The first shreds of information about a man he would probably come to know in death better than most of his friends and acquaintances knew him in life.

More telephoning; coffee and toast at his elbow while he was at it; a quick shower, shave, dress—a sombre suit and tie . . .

Penzance was about eighty miles west, almost at the toe-end of a county which vaguely resembles a foot jutting out into the Atlantic. America next stop. He recalled with affection a rosary of place names: Newlyn, Penlee, Mousehole (pronounced like *tousle*), Lamorna, Tater-du, Nanjizal . . . and that was only the coastal fringe to Land's End.

The weathermen had got it right: blustery showers out of a turbulent grey sky. When Wycliffe arrived in the town shortly after ten the godly were thinking about church and the rest were either still in bed, or meditating on what to do with a wet Sunday, or both.

He drove along the waterfront, open to the great expanse of Mount's Bay. There was the grey-green Mount of St. Michael, a tide-island, topped by its castle; the island of Ictis, where Celtic entrepreneurs were trading Cornish tin to the Greeks when Alexander was a boy. Later to become the site of a medieval monastery, now the home of an English lord.

Wycliffe drove past a toy-town dry dock and a Trinity House repair yard where great steel buoys looked absurdly self-conscious out of the water, like fat ladies indecently exposed. Before reaching the promenade he turned off in search of Lady Street, which is close by but cunningly concealed. He found the church, and the narrow street snaked uphill from there. A few doors up, police vehicles were parked on one side and on the other, despite the rain, a small crowd waited, perhaps for Godot, perhaps for the second coming. An alert copper watching them saw Wycliffe's car about to park and advanced with intent, but changed his mind.

He saluted. "Through the shop, sir."

Lady Street is in the older part of the town; both the Glynn house and their shop next door were built while Napoleon was teaching Europe how to make war; brick with granite dressings. Most of the other houses in the street are either of naked granite or hidden under stucco, some of which is ennobled by a Regency label. Altogether a mixed bag, a pleasant jumble, two, three, and four storeys high, they make interesting roof profiles and, along with shops, offices, cafés, and pubs, there is still sufficient residential usage to maintain an agreeable balance.

The Glynn bookshop was double fronted, painted olive-green

with gilded motifs. A hanging sign in the form of an open book was inscribed: "Glynn & Son. New, Second-hand, and Rare Books. Estab: 1886."

Detective Inspector Trice, the local DI, met him at the door. "He's in his office at the back, sir. The scenes-of-crime chaps are there."

Trice, like many western so-called Celts, was stocky of build with a large flat face, small features, and hazel eyes. The steady gaze from those eyes was a professional asset.

The shop belonged to another time; there was a cash desk near the door but beyond that it was divided into bays. Wycliffe was conducted down an aisle between the bays, past stairs leading up to the second-hand and rare books department.

Trice pointed to a door under the stairs. "Leads into the house, sir; it's the only communicating door."

At the back another door opened into a small office with a window to a yard which seemed to be shared with the house.

"A girl, a sort of secretary, works here," Trice said.

Glynn's office was next door, it was larger and had a door to the yard. Sergeant Fox, the scenes-of-crime officer, and his assistants were putting the room on film, preparing a scale plan, and beginning a thorough examination of everything in it. One man was going over the main surfaces with a miniature vacuum cleaner, collecting the dust into plastic bags according to its source. Another was crawling over the floor making a meticulous study of the carpet and marking his finds with little white circles. An unbiased observer might have found difficulty in distinguishing between those scientific techniques and the rituals of an African witch doctor.

Scenes-of-crime procedures rest mainly on the assumption of Locard's Exchange Principle which asserts that a criminal will always leave traces of his presence at the scene of his crime and that he will, inadvertently, take away evidence of his visit.

"There he is, sir."

Matthew Glynn was sprawled on the floor by his mahogany desk; on the desk: a telephone, an open file, a scribbling pad, an engagement diary, a whisky bottle and a couple of glasses. Wycliffe noted these things sub-consciously. He stooped over the body: the odour of stale whisky lingered. Glynn was a big man but he carried no surplus flesh; he was bald except for an exiguous fringe of greying hair; his face was long and deeply furrowed; a distinguished-looking man, a man to be reckoned with. He wore a striped shirt, a cardigan, corded trousers, matching socks, and brogue shoes.

Someone had hit him on the back of the head, a blow which had given rise to bleeding; a small area of the carpet where the head rested was encrusted with coagulated blood. The blow had not been fatal and the killer had finished his work by strangulation. The ear which could be seen was blue, so were the lips, and the tongue protruded. There were marks on the sinewy neck left by a plaited ligature. Bell-flex?

Trice said: "Odd, isn't it?"

Odd for a man to be strangled. Strangulation is a common crime, usually committed in a moment of intense passion arising from anger or sexual frenzy. Otherwise it is the work of a sadist. In either case the victim is usually a child or a woman. A strangler needs to be significantly stronger than his victim, but in this case any possibility of resistance had been ruled out by the knock on the head.

"What did the surgeon say?"

"Not much; death probably occurred late yesterday evening or early in the night: a single, stunning blow which must have caused severe concussion but wasn't fatal, followed by strangulation with a plaited ligature."

Wycliffe felt at a loss, like an actor who has anticipated his entrance by many lines in the script. It was unusual for him to arrive before his headquarters team. Now Trice was looking at him, expecting action, but what he wanted was time to take in the setting then, slowly, to learn about the man, his family, his friends . . .

He said, in order to say something: "Premeditated murder."

"That's for sure, sir. You don't pay a social call with a cudgel and a length of bell-flex in your pocket."

"Is there anybody with the family?"

"No, sir. My sergeant took a brief formal statement from Sara Glynn, the dead man's sister—she found the body—but I thought it better to leave the rest to your people—not to muddy the water. The family have been asked not to leave the house for the time being."

"How have they taken it—Glynn's death, I mean?"

Pouted lips. "Hard to say, sir. They're shocked; who wouldn't be? But I haven't seen any red eyes."

Fox, the scenes-of-crime officer, felt that he was being left out. "Look at these, sir."

He pointed to certain of the little circles which his colleague had drawn on the carpet. Wycliffe stooped and saw that each circle enclosed a faint paw mark, the marks led away from the area round the dead man's head for several feet in the direction of the door to the yard.

"A cat," Wycliffe said, obligingly perceptive.

"Exactly, sir." Fox was an oddity: very thin, with a profile like Mr. Punch. Half-glasses, habitually worn well down his nose, added to the bizarre effect. "It looks as though the creature sniffed around the dead man, stepped in the blood, then went for the door."

A question was required and Wycliffe asked it: "Was the door open or shut when the body was found?"

"It was shut, according to Sara Glynn; shut, but not locked. On the mat near the door there are cat hairs and further traces of blood. It looks as though the cat sat there for some time, waiting for someone to let it out."

"Is there a cat belonging to the house?"

"Not as far as I have been able to ascertain, sir." Sometimes Fox sounded like Jeeves.

Odd about the cat though; wherever it had come from it must have been shut in for a time. Either the killer had stayed on for some reason, ignoring the cat, or someone had opened the door, after the killer had gone, and let it out.

"The cat wasn't here when our chaps arrived this morning?"

"No, sir; I enquired."

He stood by the dead man's chair. A little more than twelve hours earlier Matthew Glynn had sat in that chair, involved in the convoluted patterns of his existence. The file on his desk containing minutes of a council committee was heavily annotated; the engagement diary was sprinkled with appointments, some of which he had kept, others he would never keep. Matthew Glynn was dead, an inanimate object which in a short time would be at the mercy of the pathologist's scalpel . . .

There must have been a visitor, possibly a member of his family; in any case someone sufficiently at home to move freely about the office, to take up a position behind the seated man so that he could strike a vicious blow. No struggle; Glynn had slipped to the floor, pushing his chair away as he fell. The murderer must have knelt beside him, taken a plaited flex from his pocket and slipped it round the neck of the unconscious man. A knot, a thin rod, even a pencil inserted in the knot, and there was a tourniquet. Simple! No strength required; a woman could have done it; a child. Wide open.

Wycliffe looked about him.

The office dated from early in the century: the mahogany desk, the wooden filing cabinet, the massive green-painted safe with its brass handle and a design in gold on the front. The desk chair swivelled on four sinuously curved wooden legs. On the wall there were framed photographs of three earlier Glynns with the dates during which they had done their stint for the firm. They impressed Wycliffe. The Glynns of today are living fossils; in this brave new world only institutions are capable of such feats of survival, and few enough of them.

Wycliffe turned to Fox: "No sign of any break-in?"

"None, sir. The exterior doors of the whole premises are provided with mortice locks and the windows are wired to an alarm system. *If* the killer did not come through from the house then Glynn must have left this door to the yard *and* the door into the back lane unsecured. *Or* he admitted the killer himself." Like Queen Victoria, Fox tended to speak in italics.

Wycliffe returned to the smaller office and Trice joined him. "Tell me about the Glynns."

Trice considered his words. "On the face of it they're a typical business family of the old school—not many of their sort left; they make their money quietly, no show, and they do their best to keep family skeletons decently locked up. Discreet—that's the word.'' Trice smiled, pleased with himself.

"What sort of man was Matthew? Well known? Well liked?"

"Well known anyway: a local businessman and a district council-lor. As to being liked, I've never heard much against him. He's made a bit of a reputation for sniffing out backstairs deals in local government and I suppose that's more likely to make him enemies than friends."

"What about the rest of the family? Is there a widow?"

Trice smoothed his double chin. "Good question, sir. The lady walked out seventeen years ago and she hasn't been seen since."

"She walked out and was untraced?"

"So it seems."

"There must have been a missing persons inquiry?"

"There was. It was before my time but I know they picked up her car, abandoned, somewhere in Exeter."

"Apart from the hypothetical widow, what about the rest of the family?"

"They had three children and all three are still living at home: Gerald, a bachelor in his late twenties, works in the business; Gina, a bit younger, also works in the shop. She's married to a chap called Morse—Barry Morse, an accountant with Mitchell and Slade. Morse is a retiring sort of chap, very musical, but they say he's a wizard with accounts. Then there's the youngest, Chris-tine, she's a student nurse at the local hospital."

"The Morses live next to the shop with the others?"

"Oh, yes; that's a biggish house next door so I don't imagine they are falling over each other. Then there's Sara, Matthew's unmarried sister, she lives there too. She seems to have taken over when Matthew's wife walked out; she's younger than Matthew—late forties—and what you might call a worthy virgin.

"Until a few months ago there was Granny Glynn—she died around Christmas, nearly ninety. Big funeral, everybody there who was anybody or wanted to be."

At the start of any case there is a flood of fact and fiction; the job is to find out which is which and whether the facts are rele-vant. In the present case Wycliffe would only gradually come to realize the full significance of what he had just been told, that Granny Glynn—a very old lady—had recently died.

"Are they still one big happy family?"

Trice grinned. "They live together anyway."

Wycliffe was juggling with names, names which, with one exception, were not yet attached to faces; the exception was the dead man. In the next few hours he would have to acquaint himself with the whole family, with their relationships in terms of both kinship and sentiment, but experience had taught him to take information in small doses.

"Let's take a look outside."

The yard was common to shop and house, paved for the most part but with a couple of flower beds and shrubs in tubs.

They went out into a narrow lane where the back doors of Lady Street confronted those of a row of houses in the next street. The lane was a track just wide enough for the refuse truck. Uniformed coppers were, as they say, "combing the area" in and out of the yards, poking about in the weedy margins of the track and turning out the contents of dustbins.

Trice said: "They're searching for the weapon—I suppose we ought to say weapons: there's the bell-wire as well as the blunt instrument. It's just possible he tossed them over a wall."

Possible, but unlikely; all the same the police had to search; no stone unturned. Soured policemen know that truth lies under the unturned stone.

"Hullo, Dippy! What do you want?"

A scrawny little man had appeared in a doorway almost opposite the Glynns'. He looked at Trice without enthusiasm. "I was out here last night and I thought maybe this gentleman would want to know what I saw."

Trice turned to Wycliffe: "Dippy Martin, sir. Dippy used to be a regular customer at our nick—specialized in ladies' handbags, but he's a reformed character now. Isn't that right, Dippy?"

"If you say so, Mr. Trice."

"Anyway, what did you see last night?"

Dippy threw away the butt of the cigarette he had been smoking. "I saw young Glynn—Gerald; he'd just put his car away in one of the lock-ups at the top of the lane and he come down to go in through the yard door but it was bolted and he couldn't. It was raining, he'd had one or two, and he was cursing fit to blister the paintwork, but in the end he give up and off he goes round the block. I s'pose he got in the front way."

"What time was this?"

"After eleven; p'raps ten or quarter past."

"Is that all?"

"No." Dippy, now sure of his ground, stopped to light another cigarette. "After that I strolled up to the corner and I hung about there for a bit. When I was coming back I saw a woman just going in."

"Into the Glynns' yard?"

"Into their yard. It was dark and she was a fair bit away so I couldn't see who it was."

"But you're sure it was a woman?"

"Unless it was a pansy in drag. No, it was a woman all right."

"What time was this?"

"Half-eleven, give or take a few minutes, sir."

"You know the Glynn women, could it have been one of them?"

"Could've bin, sir. I jest couldn't say one way or t'other."

"Did you see or hear any more after that?"

"No, sir. I was there till past midnight and I didn' see nothing more."

When they were back in the yard Wycliffe said: "I notice you didn't ask him what he was doing, hanging about in the rain."

"He was looking for his daughter. Poor old Dippy, he's not a bad sort and he's got his troubles. Cissie is feebleminded and whenever she gets loose she's off after men."

Wycliffe said: "Getting back to the Glynns: are there any other relatives living locally?"

"Two brothers: Alfred, who's older than Matthew, has the chemist's shop down the street. He's a queer one; he's unmarried and lives over his shop. As far as I know he never sees anybody but his customers and there can't be many of them. Maurice, the younger brother, has a pottery over at Trebyan, near St. Hilary— five or six miles from here. He's a widower, with a grown-up son."

"Do the brothers get on?"

Trice spread expressive hands. "I believe there's been a long-standing quarrel between Matthew and Alfred—the chemist. Until their mother died Alfred used to visit but I gather he hasn't been near the place since. And recently I've heard talk of a row between Matthew and the other brother, Maurice. It seems Matthew wanted to build houses close to his brother's pottery and, according to gossip, they nearly came to blows about it in the bookshop."

Wycliffe was used to it; lift any stone and there is life underneath and life is tension; if family quarrels were motive for murder there would be no problem of over-population.

Trice said: "Will you let me give you a bit of advice, sir?"

"Why not?"

"You haven't had much experience in this part of the world."

"I've been in the south-west long enough—you know that."

"I'm not talking about the south-west or even about Cornwall. I'm talking about Penwith; in Cornish *penwyth* means 'the extreme end.' The people here feel different—they *are* different."

Wycliffe sensed the unspoken "Thank God!"

"It's not that long since Penzance had its own schools, its own library, its own fire brigade, its own police." Spoken with nostalgic regret.

"So?"

"The real locals are suspicious of outsiders; it's been that way since the Saxons arrived—before that."

"So what should I do?"

Trice laughed. "Bear in mind that they're not just being bloody-minded."

Wycliffe heard voices coming from the shop; his team was beginning to arrive. Now he would be able to retire from centre stage and feel free to prowl at will. He went to meet Kersey: for many years the two men had worked together on most of the major cases in the police area.

Kersey said: "I've got Lucy Lane, Shaw, and Curnow with me, sir. There are three more DCs on the way. Shaw has gone along to the nick to see about organizing an Incident Room but I gather they're pushed for space so we may have to look elsewhere. I take it we shall use local talent for the house-to-house and Lucy, with Curnow, can start on the family . . ."

They discussed organization and tactics.

Premeditated murder is not usually committed by a stranger so Glynn's acquaintances, his intimates, and his family would be investigated in ascending order of importance. As always it would be a time-consuming, tedious, and delicate undertaking.

Wycliffe said: "Any news of Franks?" Franks, the pathologist.

Kersey grinned. "He expects to be here about lunchtime. He isn't pleased; he was all set to go sailing."

Wycliffe and Kersey worked well together, partly because their manners and attitudes complemented each other. On the surface Kersey was the typical cop: perhaps the type specimen of the genus Cop: hard faced and hard headed, cynical and born to the job. On the other hand Wycliffe gave the impression of a studious, mild-mannered man who had somehow—and surprisingly—found himself in the police force. Both assessments had an element of truth, no more.

Christine stood by the window of her attic room, surrounded by familiar things yet totally at a loss; her mind in turmoil. Her father was dead—murdered. She was shocked, grieved, incredulous; all that was quite genuine, but the sources of her distress went even deeper. She was trying to rid her mind of a possibility, a nagging suspicion, which she could neither face nor totally reject. Her whole world seemed to have fallen apart, yet out there, on the other side of the window panes, nothing had changed. The church tower, the bay, Newlyn, Penlee Point, looked as they had always looked, and the church bells were ringing for morning service.

When it seemed that she might remain indefinitely standing there she found herself creeping down the stairs to her father's room where there was an extension telephone, the only one where she could hope for privacy. She tried not to see the bed with its honeycomb quilt or the heavy walnut furniture, she tried to ignore the unique blend of smells which identified the room more precisely than any visual image. She went to the bureau, picked up the telephone and dialled her uncle's number. She waited until someone answered: David, thank God! If it had been her uncle she would have put the telephone down.

"It's me."

"Yes."

"You know what's happened?"

"Aunt Sara phoned Father early this morning. I'm very sorry, Chris. God! that sounds so stupid! I don't know what to say . . . I've been mooning about the house wondering if I ought to come over. I want to see you so much—"

"I don't think the police would let you in."

"Are you . . . well, are you all right?"

"I suppose so. I can't think." Her voice trembled.

"Darling!"

She was not getting to the point and at any moment somebody might pick up one of the other phones—or worse, find her in her father's bedroom. She was resolute. "How is Uncle, Dave?" And she added: "How did he take it?"

There was a pause, then the boy said: "I don't know. After Aunt Sara called he just told me what had happened and shut himself up in the stock-room. I can see him in there—not doing anything, just standing around with his hands in his pockets."

She said: "I'm coming over."

"Will they let you?"

"I shan't ask. I'll be at the hut in about an hour."

Alfred Glynn walked down Church Street oblivious of the drizzle, nearing the end of his Sunday morning constitutional which was almost as much a part of him as his pharmacy and the rooms above it where he had lived for thirty years. He walked with his eyes focused on the middle distance, a tall, shabby figure; his long black raincoat sagged at the hem and his homburg hat was frayed at the brim. He looked like a rabbi who had seen better days but he covered the ground in measured strides and with a magisterial dignity. No one who saw him pass would have guessed that his mind was in turmoil or that he doubted whether he could sustain himself until he reached his own door.

He was aware of the police cars outside his brother's house and he had to walk in the road to avoid people gathered on the pavement opposite, but his awareness had a dream-like quality, related to but not central to his inner concerns: his physical illness and mental distress.

His pharmacy was only five or six doors below the bookshop and he inserted the key in the lock of his own shop door with a sense of incredulous relief. The uniquely familiar smell of the shop enveloped and soothed him.

As a young man Alfred would have nothing to do with the family bookshop, he had wanted to be a doctor but, failing to make the grade, he trained as a pharmacist and his father had bought him an established business. The shop had changed little in the intervening years: it was shabby, congested, and stocked with remedies and palliatives, cosmetics and toiletries rarely seen elsewhere.

Alfred's clientele had dwindled, though to a few—mainly women—he was still half apothecary, half confessor: a confidant to whom they could whisper their most intimate secrets, as to a priest. The brown eyes never wavered; words, when they came, were few and lacking in any emotion. Perhaps a question or two, then: "You should see a doctor, but if you have made up your mind not to . . ." Occasionally he would say with finality: "I can do nothing for you; see a doctor or take the consequences."

He passed through the shop to the dispensary where, after much fumbling, he dosed himself with ouabain on his own pre-scription. He sat on a stool and felt his strength slowly returning; he breathed more freely, his muscles no longer seemed on the point of failing him and, after a few minutes, he felt equal to climbing the stairs to his living quarters.

In the little hall at the top of the stairs he removed his hat and coat. He called out: "It's me, darling! I'm back." There was no reply but he seemed content. He changed his shoes for slippers and slouched into the living-room muttering to himself.

For years he had repeated the formula: "I'll do nothing while Mother is alive . . ." This declaration alternated with another: "When Mother is gone, I'll kill him!" With the passage of years the words had lost their literal meaning and become no more than a soothing incantation, part of the ritual by which he cut himself off from the need to act for the future or think of the past. But his mother had been dead for four months.

Alfred was bemused, adrift; sometimes he felt that he could no longer distinguish between reality and illusion.

There were four main rooms above the shop: kitchen, living-room, and two bedrooms. The living-room looked down on the backyard and out over the grey-roofed houses, across the grey, misty sea to Newlyn and Mousehole. It was some time since the room had been cleaned; much longer since any attempt had been made at repairs or decoration: there was a damp patch on the chimney breast, paint peeled from the walls, and there was a film of grey dust on every ledge and surface. Crudely made shelves occupied much of the wall space and these were crowded with books, books which were largely anonymous because their spines had faded or were missing altogether.

For a while Alfred looked about him in vague, unfocused despair, then he went to a record player on a table by the window. From a box of records he selected one and put it on: an old Mantovani recording dominated by syrupy strings. Then, leaving the door open, he went out to the landing. He inserted a key into the lock of one of the bedroom doors and opened the door a little way. No light came from the room where the curtains must have been drawn. With his head in the gap he said in a low voice: "Are you awake, dear? . . . I've put on a record and I'll leave the doors open so that we can both listen . . . I'm going to warm a can of soup—leek and potato—and we'll have it with some of that nice crusty bread . . ."

His every movement was slow and hesitant, he was aware of a disturbing hiatus between the decision and the act; his thoughts came sluggishly and refused to follow a rational sequence. He was aware of all this but seemed powerless to change it. He went into the kitchen but almost immediately a bell rang downstairs. Someone was at the back door. He stood with a can of soup in his hand, distracted by the bell, uncertain what it was he had set out to do. The bell sounded again but he made no move. Then he heard the door being opened.

"It's me, Alfred—Sara."

Sara. He could not remember how long it was since his sister had last visited him, whether it was days, or weeks, or even months. He did not speak but went to stand at the top of the stairs, the soup can still in his hand. Sara was already half-way up. He showed no readiness to move and she had to push past him.

He had always been scared of Sara. While still in her teens she had been able to subdue him at will merely by hinting at things he preferred to forget. On an instant little humiliations and embarrassments of the past could be dredged up and given fresh currency. Without raising her voice or losing her temper she could bring him to heel.

She went through to the living-room where the record was still playing at full volume. She lifted the pick-up and the ensuing silence was dramatic.

"Do sit down, Alfred!"

Obediently he sat in his old wing-backed chair with the broken springs.

"Have the police been?"

He did not answer at once, then he said: "The police . . . I've been out."

"I know, I've been trying to get you on the telephone."

"I've been out."

"But have you seen the police?" She spoke slowly and distinctly.

He shook his head.

Sara pulled up a chair and sat opposite her brother. "You've heard about Matthew?"

He passed a thin hand over his face and said in a tired voice: "He's dead; I heard that."

"How did you hear?"

No answer. His eyes, surprisingly brown in contrast with his bleached skin, were restless and refused to meet her gaze.

"You know that he was murdered?"

A nod. It was only then that he seemed to realize he was still clutching the can of soup. Very deliberately he reached over the arm of his chair and placed it on the floor.

As though speaking to a child, Sara said: "Look, Alfred, this is important. The police will come, asking a lot of questions, and not only about what happened last night. You understand?"

Alfred's pale hands caressed the arm of his chair. "I suppose so." He seemed indifferent but, suddenly, he became animated and made as though to get up. "I must tell . . ." The words died on his lips as he caught Sara's eye and he subsided into his chair.

Sara was watching him; her brother; he was fifty-five yet he looked like an old man and his mind was wandering. Her big brother; her clearest memory of him went back to her early teens when he was a young man of twenty-one or -two.

She said: "You are a sick man, Alfred; perhaps you should have someone to look after you—"

He became agitated, leaning forward in his chair. "No, Sara! No! Please! There is nothing wrong with me and I don't want anyone in the house—anyone!" He was pleading.

"All right! All right, Alfred; we won't talk about it now but do try to compose yourself. Sit quietly for a moment."

For some time they faced each other in silence; the only sounds came from outside, from the maze of little alleys at the back. A car door slammed, a woman's voice called to her child, milk bottles rattled in a crate.

Abruptly, Alfred said: "Have you told Maurice?"

"I phoned Trebyan first thing this morning."

Another interval. Alfred seemed lost in thought, eventually he muttered to himself: "Trebyan."

"What about it?"

He looked up as though surprised to see her there. "Trebyan—you remember the little hut?"

"Of course I remember it."

"Is it still there?"

"I've no idea. Does it matter? It was all a long time ago, Alfred; when we were young."

He nodded and repeated softly: "When we were young—yes. Matthew wanted to build houses there, he would have pulled it down . . . That little hut was where my wife—"

In a level voice Sara interrupted him: "Don't be absurd, Alfred! You know very well that you never had a wife. All this brooding on the past is turning your mind. The past is gone—finished! Forget it!"

Alfred looked at her with the eyes of a frightened child.

But she went on, speaking harshly though without raising her voice. "You never had a wife, Alfred, and you were lucky; the woman you would have married was a bitch and a whore, and you know it. You've made yourself ill with self-indulgent fantasies and now this has happened. If you don't pull yourself together we shall have it all over again."

Alfred was cowering in his chair as though he was being whipped, his face covered with his hands. From time to time he made little whimpering sounds but Sara's voice continued, unemphatic but relentless . . .

CHAPTER THREE

Sunday (continued)

They found the weapon used to stun the bookseller: a piece of half-inch iron pipe about ten inches long. It was the ideal court exhibit, complete with bloodstain and a fragment of adherent skin. It had been tossed into a bed of nettles against the wall of the churchyard. Even its provenance had been established: a whole heap of such material—mostly in longer pieces—had been ripped out of a nearby house and lay, awaiting removal. Now the piece had been put into a polythene bag and given a label pending its despatch for forensic examination. Needless to say it carried no prints.

Wycliffe went in search of Sara and was received in the drawing-room.

"A worthy virgin" Trice had called her and Wycliffe saw at once what he meant. There was something essentially virginal about Sara Glynn, not the virginity of naïvety or innocence, but the soured virginity which arises from resentment of the female role. She might have been the headmistress of a certain type of girls' school, now almost extinct, or a mother superior in an enclosed order. At any rate there could be no doubt that she had found the temptations of the flesh resistible.

She wore a dove-grey Jaeger frock, discreet and asexual, but off an expensive peg. She was hollow eyed, drawn, and seemed very close to exhaustion but she had herself well in hand.

"I understand that it was you who found your brother's body?"

"Yes, and it was I who informed the police." Prompt and explicit.

"You found him in his office at shortly after six this morning?"

"That is so."

Wycliffe was gentle but persistent. "You had a reason for going there at that time?"

"I did. I woke feeling unwell and I decided to go downstairs and make myself a cup of tea. In the kitchen I noticed that there was a light in my brother's office. It was possible that he had forgotten to switch it off last night or that he was at work early, but it was also possible that there had been an intruder. I went there to find out."

"You couldn't see into the office from the kitchen?"

"No, the curtains were drawn."

Sara Glynn sat opposite Wycliffe in the big, rather gloomy room with its dark wallpaper, over-varnished oil paintings in gilt frames, and leather-upholstered chairs.

There was something about the woman which brought out the official streak in Wycliffe and with it the pompous, well-rounded phrases: "I'm afraid that we shall have to look into your brother's affairs and into his relationships both inside and outside the family. Some of the questions that are asked may seem impertinent, but you may be assured . . ." The official blend of stimulant and tranquilizer.

She shifted her position and adjusted the fine wool of her skirt over her bony knees. Despite her tiredness her movements were deliberate, unhurried, and self-absorbed; like a cat. When her attention returned to Wycliffe it was almost as though she found it an effort to recall what they were talking about. She said: "Of course it goes without saying that you will receive full co-operation from the family."

Wycliffe was well aware that it did not "go," with or without saying. As far as Sara was concerned he would hear only what she considered fit for him to know.

"Perhaps you will tell me something about last night, how you spent the evening, whether you noticed anything unusual. You have an evening meal?"

"At 6:30."

"So we will start there. Everybody was present at the meal?"

"Yes."

"What happened afterwards?"

She pursed her lips and considered. "My niece Gina helped me with the washing-up. The woman who comes in goes at five. Afterwards I went to my room and spent the evening reading and writing letters."

"You spent the evening in your bedroom?"

"No, Chief Superintendent; I have a sitting-room as well as a bedroom upstairs."

Every word seemed to have been crafted and polished before it was allowed to escape through her discriminating lips.

"You saw or heard nothing unusual?"

"Nothing."

"Does your room overlook the back or front of the house?"

"The front."

"You are quite sure that you did not go out at all last evening?"

"Quite sure."

"When you went to your brother's office this morning was there a cat in the room?"

"A cat? No."

"You are saying that you did not see your brother alive again after the meal you had together yesterday evening. Is that so?"

She lowered her eyes and her voice. "That is correct."

It was like filling in the blank spaces on a form and equally unprofitable. More than that, she was lying; somewhere along the line, and perhaps more than once, she had found it necessary to lie. He was sure of it but there was no point in putting on pressure until he had more to go on. He changed the subject.

"You had three brothers, Miss Glynn: Alfred, Matthew, and Maurice. One would have expected that Alfred, as the eldest, would have taken over the family firm or that it would have been left to the four of you jointly."

"Alfred very much wanted to be a doctor and Father encouraged him. When it became obvious that he would not be successful he decided to train as a pharmacist and Father set him up in business."

There was an answer for everything. Clearly all things worked together for good in this family where friction was as rare as in a well-oiled machine.

"And Maurice?"

"Maurice, as a young man, had a strong antipathy for business; he went to an art college and after . . ." She hesitated, searching for the acceptable phrase. "After some false starts he set up as a potter at Trebyan in St. Hilary—a property which belongs to the family. His work is becoming well known and he is able to live comfortably."

"Your father financed him?"

Did Sara allow a slight irritation to show? At any rate she did not answer at once and Wycliffe had to insist. "I'm afraid that such questions will have to be answered, Miss Glynn; if not by you, then by others."

"All right; I will tell you. My father provided Maurice with a capital sum and leased him the property he now occupies at a nominal rental." Her look clearly said: "That must surely satisfy you!"

It did not. "When your father died—how many years ago?"

"My father died in 1977."

"So at that time the freehold of the property leased to your brother must have passed to someone else."

"Under my father's will that part of his property went to my brother Matthew."

"Your mother died quite recently, was she not involved in any of these dispositions?"

A downturn of the lips: "Glynn women have never figured in wills; it has always been assumed that the men would look after them along with their other properties."

Interesting. The first intimation of discord, even of bitterness.

The room was depressing: the single window looked out on the narrow street; there were net curtains as well as heavy, red velvet drapes drawn half-way across. Yet one was aware of everything that went on outside, of voices, of footsteps, of whatever traffic there might be.

She waited unruffled for his next question; a woman distressed but confident in her ability to handle any situation.

"Are either of your brothers married, Miss Glynn?"

"Alfred is not; he lives alone, over his shop. Maurice is a widower and has a son, David, who is twenty."

"Presumably they know what has happened?"

"I have just come back from talking to Alfred and I telephoned Maurice." A moment of hesitation, then: "I think you should know that Alfred is a sick man; he has a heart condition . . ." It was clear that she had not yet made her point. "He is also a little eccentric, sometimes very odd, probably through living so much alone . . . I hope that you will not think it necessary to harass him."

"I'll remember what you say, Miss Glynn. There is just one other matter on which I shall be grateful for information. I understand that about seventeen years ago your sister-in-law walked out of her home and did not return."

"So?"

"At that time your younger niece must have been still an infant."

"Christine was two years old. Gina was eight, Gerald eleven."

"It seems very remarkable that a woman would walk out, leaving her children like that."

"Inez, my sister-in-law, was a very remarkable woman."

"Was there another man?"

"I presume so."

"You don't know?"

A slight lift of the shoulders.

"Was there a crisis in the marriage before she left?"

"No, there was no crisis." A small smile. "Nothing disturbed the even tenor of our days. Inez left, ostensibly to spend Sunday with a woman friend, and she did not come back. They found her car abandoned in Exeter."

"Your parents were alive then; what was their attitude?"

She considered her answer. "My father was entirely pragmatic in his response to all situations, even the most distressing. He believed, as I do, that people cannot be changed, that one must learn to cope with them as they are."

"And your mother?"

"Mother was naturally very distressed."

Sara straightened her skirt once more. "That is all I can tell you, Mr. Wycliffe, because it is all there is to tell. I have been frank because there is no purpose in your people hunting for family skeletons which do not exist."

He went out into the passage and through the communicating door into the shop. Voices came from the direction of the offices and he found Fox expostulating with a tall youngish man, a Glynn without doubt and the heir apparent.

"I want to see my father and your man here won't let me. I've a right—"

Fox said: "Mr. Gerald Glynn, sir. I wouldn't let him through without your authority."

Wycliffe was soothing. "Well, now I'm here, you can come in with me, Mr. Glynn."

There was likely to be more interest in a member of the family who seemed to have come to the boil than in Sara who would cost time and patience to bring to blood heat. Wycliffe led the way into Glynn's office where one of the scenes-of-crime team was still at work. Wycliffe stooped and lifted the sheet which covered the body.

Gerald stood, looking down at his father, his face expression-less. After a moment or two he asked: "Did that knock on the head kill him?" He added with a hint of apology: "I don't under-stand about this sort of thing."

"No, your father was strangled."

"It must've been a pretty powerful bloke who did that; Father was no weakling."

"We think that he was first stunned by the blow on the head."

"Ah! So anybody could've done it?"

"So it seems."

"A woman?"

"Yes, but why do you ask?"

Gerald said nothing but his gaze shifted to the desk, to the whisky bottle and glasses. "Somebody got him pissed, I expect; it wasn't difficult." He sounded tolerant, almost affectionate.

Back in the outer office Wycliffe said: "A few questions while you are here, Mr. Glynn . . ."

They sat down. Gerald was subdued. He said: "I could have seen him this morning before your lot arrived but I funked it."

Wycliffe nodded. "That is understandable. Now for my ques-tions. It seems that your father willingly admitted his killer. Can you suggest any visitor who might have arrived, late in the evening, and been admitted like that?"

"Anybody."

"Anybody?"

"That's what I said. If you're in politics you have to cope with two sorts of people, the ones you can use, and the ones who want to use you. Father made sure he was well acquainted with both sorts. He kept his ear to the ground and he spent a lot of time in his office after hours. All sorts would turn up for a little chat." Gerald smiled. "The old man was a damn good listener when it suited him and he knew the right questions. I can speak from experience."

"Presumably he would be alone with his visitor during these sessions?"

"Of course! People likely to provide him with ammunition for his little campaigns wouldn't appreciate an audience any more than they'd want to be seen tripping up the steps of the council offices to some bloody committee room."

"Wasn't it unwise of him to keep open house like that, with direct access to his office from a back lane?"

"Probably, but he's been doing it for years."

"Is it possible, in your view, that he might have been killed because of his 'little campaigns' as you call them?"

Gerald was contemptuous. "These things are only shadowboxing, overgrown schoolboys sparring; they never come to much. The alternatives are bowls, golf, or chasing widow women."

"There was a cat in your father's office last night."

"That doesn't surprise me; the old man was fond of cats so Sara decided to be allergic to cat's fur and Father encouraged the neighbourhood moggies into his office with kitchen scraps. Ronnie Swayne's—from next door—a monstrous beast, is one of the regulars."

Gerald pulled out a crushed packet of cigarettes from a trouser pocket and lit one. He took a brief draw then fingered tobacco grains from his lips.

Wycliffe changed the subject. "Your father must have had many acquaintances in business and in his council work, but did he have any close friends?"

"Old ferret-face next door—Ronnie Swayne; he deals in stamps, medals, and coins. Then there's Mike Doble who keeps the wine shop farther up. They meet fairly often to play chess."

"Here?"

"Swayne's place; he lives over his shop. Father was there last night."

"Three of them play chess?"

"Don't ask me; I never mastered Snakes and Ladders. Anyway Mike is ill in hospital at the moment and unlikely to play chess for a bit."

"How did you spend yesterday evening, Mr. Glynn?"

"At the Grantham in St. Ives, playing snooker."

"At what time did you get home?"

"About 11:15, give or take a few minutes."

"You were driving?"

"I was."

"What did you do with your car?"

"I keep it in one of the lock-ups at the top of the back lane."

"And did you come into the house by the back or the front door?"

"The front. I didn't have any choice; the yard door was bolted. I had to walk round the bloody block."

"Is that usual?"

"No, of course it isn't! I thought Father had done it out of spite. We haven't been getting on too well lately."

Wycliffe spoke to the scenes-of-crime officer: "When you arrived this morning was the yard door bolted?"

"Yes, sir."

"Check to see if that was the position when our chaps first came on the scene."

Gerald said: "I suppose somebody could have been in there doing the old man while I was trying to get in. But if the door was bolted this morning . . ."

"You were seen trying to get in last night, Mr. Glynn."

"I know; Dippy Martin was out looking for Cissie."

"And some time after you went round to the front of the house a woman was seen to go in."

"A woman? I don't get it."

"That is what Martin says; he was some distance away at the time and wasn't able to see who it was."

"You've lost me."

"Is there anybody who might have had a serious grudge against your father?"

Gerald shrugged. "Sounds a bit hyped up put like that but he and Uncle Alfred had a long-running feud."

"What about?"

Suddenly Gerald became vague. "A quarrel about some girl, I think. It's been that way ever since I can remember. Something from the hot, heady days of youth when the sap was rising. There were never any dramatic confrontations; they just didn't have anything to do with each other."

"Your uncle is the pharmacist, down the street?"

"Yes, but you can't seriously think . . . He's a sick man and he's . . . I mean you only have to look at him. He couldn't swot a fly with a rolled-up newspaper."

"And your father's other brother—Maurice, with the Trebyan pottery at St. Hilary—was there any friction there?"

Gerald ran his fingers through his dark hair. "Christ! You make us sound like the Mafia or something. We're an ordinary family with the usual family squabbles."

"But you haven't answered my question."

"Well, there's a spot of bother at the moment. Father owns the pottery, a bit of scrubland around it and a couple of small fields. All that's left of the Glynn acres." Gerald grinned. "The Glynns were farmers once upon a time. Actually, the family lived at Trebyan up to a few months before I was born, then they moved next door to be near the shop."

"So what's the trouble about?"

"Just that Father wants—wanted to build houses on the scrub and on one of the fields. He was after outline planning and thought he was going to get it. Maurice is raising hell—spoliation of the countryside, damage to the rural environment, forcible eviction of rabbits—you name it." He looked at Wycliffe with a sheepish smile. "Maurice and young David are 'Greens' and into organic vegetables, goats' milk, and yoghurt." He became serious.

"You can't see people like that . . ." He nodded towards the adjoining office.

In his own way Gerald was more skilful at whitewashing the family than his Aunt Sara.

"Well, thank you, Mr. Glynn, that's all for the moment but I may have more questions for you later."

When Gerald had gone Wycliffe joined Fox in Matthew's office.

"You were asking about the yard door, sir; it was bolted when the local police arrived this morning."

"By the way, any prints on the whisky glasses?"

"The deceased's on one, the other has been wiped clean."

Wycliffe stood by the window, looking across the yard to the back of the house. He could see the back door and what was, presumably, the kitchen window. Sara said that she was standing at that window when she noticed the light in the office. At six in the morning it would be daylight, and with the curtains drawn in the office . . .

Wycliffe left the office and walked the length of the dimly lit shop. The window blinds were down and he had a feeling that he was behind the scenes in a theatre. The bay to his left was labelled "Fiction A–H," and to his right was the cash desk looking much the same as it must have done on the day the shop was first opened.

He could just read the faded inscription painted above the window: "Glynn's Circulating Library. Established 1886." (When all the women were reading Mrs. Henry Wood, and Marie Corelli was about to burst upon a waiting world.) Four generations of Glynns, and the fourth of the dynasty had got himself murdered in his own office; no heat-of-the-moment crime either, but a carefully planned murder executed in cold blood out of hatred, or fear, or obsessive greed.

The business of the yard door was puzzling; it was bolted at 11:15 and mysteriously unbolted later so that an unidentified woman was able to enter at about 11:30, but bolted again when the police arrived some time after six in the morning. Then there was the cat . . . and Sara . . .

"Second-hand and Rare Books." Wycliffe went upstairs to look. As always he was nosing out the territory like a dog in a new home; no objective in view. The upper floor was divided into two by a wooden screen with hammered-glass panels and a door bearing a notice: "For access to the rare books section please apply at the desk."

Wycliffe browsed among the second-hands. Along with scores of authors of whom he had never heard he found forgotten friends: Hugh Walpole, John Galsworthy, and the redoubtable Mazo de la Roche, captivator of millions who would now be devotees of TV soaps . . . He must have been more sentimental and less cynical then. But this was no trip down memory lane and there was nothing to see but books. He was on the point of returning downstairs when he noticed that the door to the rare book section was not quite closed. Out of curiosity he pushed it open. The space devoted to rare books was very much smaller than that given to the second-hand. A few bookcases with glazed doors were arranged around the walls leaving a central space for a table and chairs. The floor was carpeted and the impression was one of a small library in a rather run-down country house.

If he had not actually gone into the room he would not have seen Gina; she was standing against one of the bookcases hidden from him by the open door.

"Mrs. Morse? . . . Chief Superintendent Wycliffe."

"I know." The door of the bookcase was open but there were no other signs of how she had been engaged. For some reason though she looked guilty. "I had to be occupied; it's so demoralizing just waiting around. It's my job to keep a check on the stock and it seemed a good chance to get something done . . ." She was flustered.

Gina was an attractive young woman, on the plump side, oval face, dark hair and eyes, a pale skin, and freckles. At the age of seven he had fallen in love with a schoolteacher like her.

"So this is the rare books section." To say something.

"That's what we call it but most of the books are not all that rare. We go in mainly for first editions of the classics but we do have some rather nice botanical books, floras mostly, sought after for their plates . . . We make a thing of local-interest books . . ."

She was over-anxious, talking too much.

"Somebody will be asking you questions more formally but perhaps you could tell me if you went out at all last evening?"

She seemed surprised, perhaps relieved by the question. "No, I was in all the evening."

"Do you know about your sister?"

"Christine went to a play at St. John's Hall; she came in at about half-past ten."

"And your aunt tells me that she spent the whole evening in her room. I ask because a witness claims to have seen a woman entering your yard by the yard door at about 11:30."

She shook her head. "There must be some mistake. Apart from anything else that door was bolted then, my brother couldn't get in."

"Is it possible that your father had a woman visitor? I mean, is it possible that he had some emotional involvement outside the family?"

Gina looked blank then understanding dawned. "You mean a woman!" She laughed shortly. "Father had more than enough of women in the house and the business."

Wycliffe said: "Do you remember your mother, Mrs. Morse?"

"Of course I remember her; I was eight when she left."

"And you've never seen or heard of her since?"

"No."

"Surely your mother's absence must have given rise to a great deal of discussion and speculation in the family—at the time and afterwards."

"If so, it was a case of 'not in front of the children.'"

"But since you've been grown up?"

She frowned. "It's hard to explain. There is very little discussion about anything in our family—the excuse was that one mustn't upset Granny, but I think it's a Glynn thing; cut discussion to a minimum, especially of unpleasant things, and perhaps they'll go away."

Wycliffe stood, irresolute, wondering how best to turn this chance encounter to advantage. "Your grandmother died four months ago; has her death had much effect on family relationships?"

It was clear that she saw the drift of his question but her answer was simple: "Granny seemed to exercise a sort of spell over her sons, her husband too, I think. I suppose the only obvious change since her death is that we no longer have our Wednesday sessions."

"What were they?"

She smiled. "Old-fashioned shops like ours still have half-day closing. We close on Wednesday afternoons and every Wednesday Maurice and Alfred would come here for a sort of high tea, presided over by Granny."

"Even though the brothers didn't get on together."

"Oh, Granny wasn't supposed to know about that. If she did, it was never admitted."

Wycliffe was apologetic. "I hope these questions won't seem offensive but we need to know as much as possible about the family. How do you remember your mother? As affectionate—loving—or was your relationship with her, say, less intimate?"

The question disturbed her and she took time to answer. "I suppose you need to know these things . . . My mother wasn't demonstrative." She hesitated. "I never remember being hugged. On the other hand she was never hard on us and never unsympathetic; she looked after us, made sure we were properly fed and clothed, that we went to bed at a reasonable time —all that sort of thing." Another reflective pause. "No one could say she wasn't a good mother."

"Looking back, does it surprise you that she left when she did?"

"Yes, it does." With emphasis.

"You were aware of no special crisis? No rows?"

"No, none." She looked at him in frank enquiry. "Does that tell you what you want to know?"

"Yes, it does, and I'm grateful, but I have one more question: Was your Aunt Sara able, in some degree, to fill your mother's place?"

She thought for some time before saying: " 'In some degree' puts it quite well."

"Were you harshly treated?"

"No." She hesitated again. "Perhaps the impression I'm giving isn't quite fair to Sara; after all, she didn't ask for the job."

Wycliffe walked downstairs into the gloomy shop. A family affair. All of them at least as concerned to limit the damage as to assist the inquiry. But who could blame them? He was beginning to get to know them as individuals and to glimpse their relationships but he could never be more than the outsider looking in. He was becoming increasingly conscious of the existence of something at the core—in fact, a suspicion, a threat, which must at all costs be shielded from his probes.

It was after one. Self-absorbed and brooding, he crossed the street, oblivious of the watchers, and entered the pub opposite. He elbowed his way to the bar and ordered a lager and a ham sandwich. If he was the cynosure of all eyes he didn't notice and in his present mood he wouldn't have been troubled if he had.

Although the little hut at Trebyan was only a couple of hundred yards from the house and the pottery it was over the slope of the hill and hemmed in by gorse and hawthorn: a single large room with a verandah, built of lap boarding, raised on a brick base and set in the side of the hill. From the verandah the only sign of human habitation was the tower of St. Hilary church rising out of the trees half a mile away.

Christine reached the hut from the road by a steep track through the scrub and so avoided the house. David was waiting.

"Chris!" He took her in his arms and hugged her, breathless. "I was afraid they wouldn't let you come."

A kiss, and she moved away. "I didn't ask; I told Gina where I was going but I'd better not stay too long."

They stood side by side, arms resting on the verandah rail. Although it was overcast with rain threatening, opportunist bumble bees were making the most of the gorse flowers.

David said: "You don't have to say it, Chris; I know . . . It's worrying me too." He put his hand to his head. "God! I never manage to say anything properly! I meant what's worrying you as well as the awful thing that happened to your father . . ."

At twenty he had not quite grown out of the gangling stage either in the control of his long limbs or in the expression of his most deeply felt thoughts and emotions.

"If only Dad hadn't lost his temper with Uncle Matt like that nobody would even think of it . . ."

Christine put her hand on his arm. "Dave! As far as we know nobody has, but we mustn't be afraid to talk about what worries us. We're more likely to see how silly it is. Nobody who knew Uncle Maurice could possibly believe that he could do such a thing. The two of them had a row about building houses here. All right! Perhaps they would have gone to court about it, but that doesn't mean that either of them . . ."

David said: "I keep telling myself that but it doesn't stop me worrying."

They remained standing close, gazing out over the valley. Finally, speaking in a low voice, the boy said: "There's something you don't know: Dad told me this morning that he was in bed when I got home last night."

"Well, he often is, isn't he?"

"Not last night; I heard him come in a long time after I went to bed. I don't know what time it was but it must have been late."

"Did he have the Land Rover?"

"No, I would have heard that."

"So he was walking."

"There's an old bike he sometimes uses."

"You haven't asked him about it?"

He turned towards her. "How could I?"

"No, sorry! . . . Where is he now?"

"I left him in the house; I said I was going to see to the goats."

It was very quiet, not a sound anywhere; the cloud cover was beginning to thin and there was watery sunshine.

"He told the police he was already in bed when I got home."

"They've been here?"

"A detective and a uniformed bobby just after you rang. They didn't stay long and they were very polite. Dad told them he went for a drink to the pub at Goldsithney, that he left at about nine and came straight home."

In a voice that made it sound like an article of faith, Christine said: "We both know that your father didn't kill mine so why he was late and why he didn't tell the police about it doesn't matter."

"I love you, Chris."

She faced him. "You only know what your father told you."

He took her in his arms but she separated from him. "Not now, love; I must get back. But Dave . . ."

He turned to her, questioning.

"Remember, whatever happens we are still us."

When Wycliffe returned to the bookshop Dr. Franks's Porsche had joined the line of vehicles down one side of the street and it was raining. Franks had just arrived with his secretary and was still in the shop.

"Oh, there you are, Charles! Have you had lunch?"

"Of a sort."

"Lucky you! Liz, here, bought me a ham sandwich on the way down: ghastly! You've met Liz, of course."

"No."

"*Really?*"

The pathologist's secretaries followed one another in bewildering succession. Usually Franks was elegantly dressed in fine worsted with a silk shirt; today he wore a denim overall. "Liz and I were going sailing, damnit! First time out for the season."

He was walking in and out of the bays, studying the bookshelves as though that was what he had come for. "This is a good bookshop, Charles." He spoke as a connoisseur might speak of a cheese or a wine. "When I was a boy my parents had a bookshop like this in Plymouth. They had second-hand books upstairs too. I used to spend Saturday mornings up there reading Havelock Ellis and Marie Stopes until the old man tumbled to it. Father was an old-time Methodist; sex and the devil were one. Perhaps he was right.

"Well, where is the *corpus delicti*, old chap?"

The ritual began. Franks made his preliminary examination of the body, dictating brief comments to his secretary. The body was moved into fresh positions with Fox recording the whole process on film.

"Rigor is almost complete. Taking one thing with another: body temperature, ambient temperature, the fact that Saturn is in the ascendant and it's Sunday, I'd say he's been dead up to eighteen hours, probably not less than fourteen, that puts it between nine and one last night. Does that square with anything you know?"

"It would have a job not to."

Wycliffe was always irritated by Franks, by his flamboyant and casual approach to death. He went on: "I would like the contents of his pockets now; his clothes will go to Forensic."

"You don't need me to tell you that he was stunned first, then strangled."

"The weapon used for the blow?"

Franks peeled off his surgical gloves. "I don't know. Perhaps a piece of metal piping with a bit of a ragged edge."

"How about this?" Wycliffe pointed to Exhibit A.

Franks grinned. "Looks all right to me. It seems to have struck edge-on as though the blow nearly missed. That caused more bleeding than our friend probably bargained for. I expect he/she wanted to avoid being spattered."

"And did he/she succeed?"

"Perhaps. The blood would trickle, not come in spurts."

"What about the ligature? Anything enlightening about that?"

"Not really. Plaited flex certainly but it probably had a large knot or something to increase pressure in the region of the larynx."

"So we are looking for someone who knew his business."

"Someone who came fully prepared anyway."

The body was moved once more to make the pockets accessible and Fox searched them—there were only those in his trousers; he was wearing a cardigan in place of a jacket. The contents were predictable: a leather key-fold, a couple of pounds in coin, and a handkerchief. No safe key; it would have been too large for the key-fold.

Franks said: "Well, I'm off, Charles. Shift him when you like but the sooner you get him over to me the better. They tell me there's still a chance of a decent lunch at the hotel on the prom."

Wycliffe saw Franks and his secretary off at the shop door. Misty rain, or Sunday lunch, or sheer boredom had dispersed the spectators and Lady Street was deserted.

CHAPTER FOUR

Sunday (continued)

The family had gathered in the kitchen for a late lunch made up of left-overs. There was no appliance in the kitchen less than thirty years old; the walls were painted cream with a green dado and the red-tiled floor was scrubbed every Friday by the cleaning woman. The wall clock had "Glynn Books" lettered on its face and had been transferred to the kitchen from the shop in some major upheaval of the past. They had eaten what there was, sitting or standing around; only Sara sat at the table.

Gina said: "I'll make some coffee—or tea, if anybody wants it."

Nobody spoke and she went on: "Tea or coffee, Gerald?"

Her brother was standing by the window, looking across the yard to the single-storey extension which housed his father's office. He turned to her. "What? . . . All right, if you like. I'll have coffee."

"Barry?"

Gina's husband was perched on a stool by the refrigerator. To his straw-coloured hair and blue eyes he added an obvious desire to please, at least to be agreeable, attributes which were rare amongst the Glynns. In zoological terms Barry was a commensal— a tolerated intruder from another species.

He seemed startled by his wife speaking his name. "Yes—sorry, what is it?"

"Do you want coffee or tea?" Gina enunciated the words as though speaking to a backward child.

"Yes, yes please; I'll have coffee if you're making some."

Gina filled the kettle and laid out cups and saucers. In the brooding silences the ticking of the clock seemed to become louder. They were trapped in each other's company, each one wanting to break away, to do anything rather than stay there together, but none of them would risk being thought unfeeling, or odd. It was the same with talk: what is an acceptable subject of conversation when one of the family has been murdered and the police are in the house?

Only Sara seemed composed and judicial; looking directly at Gerald she said: "The police have only just started their questioning; I think we should be very careful about what we say to them. It will be all too easy to raise in their minds questions which have nothing to do with your father's death."

And when they had drunk their coffee it was Sara who broke the spell. She got up from her chair. "Well, I've got things to do."

As she was leaving, Gerald said: "Shouldn't you tell me what it is I'm supposed to keep quiet about?"

Sara looked at her nephew but said nothing.

When the door had closed behind her Gerald waited, his eye on the door, as though to make sure that she was not coming back. Gina said: "Why be so bloody-minded, Gerald?"

Gerald countered with a question of his own: "Has the Big Chief grilled you yet?"

"I've spoken to him."

"And?"

"He asked me what I was doing last night, and then one or two questions about Mother."

"About Mother? What about her?"

"He wanted to know if, looking back, I was surprised that she'd left. I said that I was."

Gerald said: "My God! He intends to stir with a big spoon!" And immediately changed the subject. "When I got home last night and found the yard door bolted I thought the old man had deliberately locked me out but the police reckon that whoever killed Father was with him then—while I was banging on the door, trying to get in."

Gina was incredulous. "You're saying they think the man . . . the man who killed Father locked himself in?"

"Why not? He wouldn't want to be disturbed and all he had to do to get out was draw the bloody bolt."

"You think that's what happened?"

"I've no idea but I'm beginning to wonder if the cops don't have another idea. If the door was still bolted when they arrived this morning—"

"Was it?"

"I don't know, but if it was I think they're going to get round to some really nasty questions."

Barry had been sitting, hunched up on his stool, his heels caught in the crossbar, now he became agitated. "You're not saying they might think it was one of us? They couldn't! It's too fantastic!"

Gerald was patronizing. "You'll be surprised what nasty minds some of these coppers have, Barry. They're not all like your PC Palmer, singing Schubert to well-heeled geriatrics in your Sunday concerts."

Gina, in a bored voice, said: "You really are a tailor-made bastard, Gerald."

Gerald went on as though she had not spoken. "One other thing they'll want to know is the real reason why Sara was in Father's office at just after six this morning."

Christine had been telling herself: "This isn't something I've read in the newspapers, this is happening to us! My father has been murdered and my uncle . . . Yet we sit here drinking coffee and . . . and talking as if . . ." She said aloud, with an edge to her voice: "What are you saying, Gerald? Aunt Sara wasn't feeling well; she came downstairs and saw a light in Father's office . . ."

Gerald was gentle with her. "It was daylight at six, Chris, and the curtains were drawn in Father's office—like now. See for yourself: could you tell from here if there was a light on?"

After Franks had left, Wycliffe went to pay a courtesy call at the local station. The skies were clearing. The weather, fickle over this western peninsula, makes mock of the forecasters. As he walked up Lady Street the sun broke through and he was able to take his first leisurely look at the pleasing medley of styles, periods, and usage. The pavements were narrow, granite slabs set at ankle-wrenching angles, so that in the Sabbath quiet it was pleasanter to walk in the road.

"M. Doble. Wine Merchant"—presumably the other chess player, now in hospital. A freshly painted shop front with shining glass and a window full of bottles. The windows over the shop were discreetly curtained so it was likely that whatever Dobles there might be lived over the shop.

At the nick he found a reception committee from the press. Even reporters are sluggish on Sundays.

"I'll arrange a press briefing as soon as I have a base and something to say; meanwhile, all I can tell you is that early this morning Matthew Glynn, the bookseller, was found dead in his office in circumstances suggesting foul play."

"How did he die?"

"I haven't had the pathologist's report but the indications are that he was strangled after being stunned by a blow to the head."

A wizened little man Wycliffe had known of old said: "Somebody didn't like him. Are you expecting to make an arrest shortly?"

"No."

"What was the motive?"

"I've no idea, and that is the truth."

"Anything taken?"

"Not as far as I know."

"A break-in?"

"There were no signs of a forced entry."

When they were satisfied that there was no more to be got they let him go.

He found Kersey, sitting at the desk in a borrowed upstairs office surrounded by house-to-house reports prepared on the premises. Kersey said: "They're doing all they can but there's really no way they can fit us in here for any length of time. Shaw is after an available property which Trice suggested. It's just across the road from the bookshop, down a little alley; about eight hundred square feet in three rooms, up one flight of stairs."

"You've seen it?"

"I think it should suit."

"Good enough."

DS Shaw, who, amongst other things, acted as the squad's quartermaster, would see to the hiring, and the fitting out of the rooms with equipment from central stores.

"Anything in the reports?"

In a symbolic gesture of renunciation Kersey pushed his cigarette pack farther away. "As usual, ninety percent waste paper, but there is something on Sara. A witness claims to have seen her in Alexandra Road last night at about 11:15."

"Reliable?"

"Our chap thought so."

"And that ties in with what Dippy Martin had to say about a woman entering by the Glynns' back door at around 11:30."

In movements which could have been those of a somnambulist Kersey had retrieved his cigarettes and was placing one between his lips while feeling in his pockets for a lighter. "You want me to follow this up?"

Wycliffe said: "I'll think about it; we need to be careful with Sara. Anything else in the reports?"

"Only gossip. It's common talk that Alfred is around the twist and that he's got worse recently, since his mother died. They say he's been stopped from dispensing NHS prescriptions."

Kersey stroked his rubbery nose between finger and thumb, a sure sign of cerebration. "How do you see it, sir? A family thing or an outsider?"

Wycliffe was dismissive. "How can anybody see it? Franks says Glynn died between nine and one, he might as well have said last night sometime. It's open to the whole family plus any outsider with a sufficient grudge against Glynn.

"The only indication we have is that somebody seems to have drawn the bolt on the yard door between Gerald failing to get in at 11:15, and the mystery woman succeeding at 11:30. It's tempting to think that the killer made his getaway during that fifteen minutes."

"Or that somebody in the house wanted to give that impression."

"Guessing games!"

"Now it looks as though the mystery woman could have been Sara."

Wycliffe sighed. "It's all speculative. I doubt if we shall get far by concentrating on opportunity; it's motive that matters in this case."

"The brothers weren't exactly fraternal."

"No, but I've yet to come across anything that looks like a motive for murder. Anyway, I'm off to talk to this character Swayne. You see what you can do with Alfred—better still, let Lucy Lane try; the feminine touch."

Kersey called after him: "Shaw has fixed us up at the hotel on the prom—is that all right?"

"Sounds luxurious. I wonder if our paymasters will stand for it."

"They're still on out-of-season rates."

Next door to the Glynn shop there was a narrow frontage like a slice cut from a larger premises: two storeys, one room width, with an attic. The shop window was tiny and covered by a metal grille. In it coins and medals were set out on faded velvet pads and, at the back, there were cards of stamps displayed under amber polythene to protect them from the light. A discoloured printed card read: "Collections Valued and Purchased."

Ronnie Swayne: probably the last person to see Glynn alive apart from his killer.

Watched by the group of people opposite, Wycliffe pressed the doorbell and waited. After an interval he heard someone coming downstairs, bolts were drawn and the door was opened by a little man with freckles and vestiges of red hair.

"Mr. Swayne?"

"You're from the police." It was a statement.

"Chief Superintendent Wycliffe."

"I'm glad you've come."

The door did not lead into the shop as Wycliffe had expected but into a minute hall with the shop door on the right, and stairs leading up. Swayne secured the door and led the way upstairs to a sizeable but cluttered room at the front of the house, overlooking the street.

Swayne wore rust-coloured trousers and a matching pullover, his movements were erratic, rapid yet precise, so that Wycliffe was reminded of a little red monkey.

"Please sit down . . . Drink? . . . No? Smoke if you want to
. . . I'm glad you've come, I was thinking of getting in touch. I
had one of your chaps here this morning asking questions but I
wanted to talk to someone in authority."

On a desk by the window a tray of stamps was in process of
being sorted; there were bookshelves, a cabinet of shallow drawers
presumably for coins, a safe, a filing cabinet; journals and cata-
logues were piled on the floor and, incongruously, a pier table and
a French commode stood against one wall looking uncomfortable.
The room was untidy, dusty, and much used.

Wycliffe put on his cud-chewing look and settled comfortably in
his chair. "It seems likely that you were the last person to see
Glynn alive, apart from his murderer, but at the moment I am
more interested in what you can tell me about him—the sort of
man he was—and about his friends and his enemies as far as you
can. You've known him a long time?"

"Pretty well all my life. When I was young my father kept an
antiques shop where the restaurant is now, so we weren't far from
the bookshop; the two families were on friendly terms and I was at
grammar school with the Glynn boys. Matt and I were the same
age within a month but Alfred was two or three years older and
Maurice quite a bit younger. But the Glynns didn't actually come
to live next to their shop until about the time Matthew got married. Before that they lived out at Trebyan—where Maurice's pottery is now."

"Can you suggest any reason why anyone might have wanted to
kill Matthew?"

Swayne was emphatic. "None! Matt wasn't the sort of man to
antagonize people. I know he made the sparks fly sometimes in
council committees but most of that was good humoured."

Wycliffe's manner was easy, conversational. "I've heard that he
wasn't on speaking terms with Alfred and that the feud—whatever it was—goes back many years . . ."

A quick look from the sharp little eyes. "You don't imagine that
Alfred—"

Wycliffe cut him short. "I don't imagine anything, Mr. Swayne;
I'm trying to find out as much as possible about the people concerned and I have to start somewhere."

"Yes, of course." Swayne took a small cigar from a box near his chair. "You don't mind? . . . You won't join me?" He went through the ritual of lighting the cigar and took a first luxurious puff before continuing: "It's not easy to put this sort of thing in proper perspective." A brief laugh. "Family feuds are hell; they don't have much logic."

Wycliffe said nothing and his expression remained bland, almost sleepy.

"Well, Matt and Alfred had very different temperaments. Alfred, as the elder, was expected to follow father in the business but he jibbed; he wanted to be a doctor. To cut a long story short, he couldn't make the grade so he ended up as a pharmacist in the business his father bought for him as a going concern. I'm pretty sure, in the way these things work, that Alfred felt he had made the wrong choice and, illogically, held it against Matthew. But that was only the start."

The door of the room opened a little way and a large tabby cat insinuated itself through the gap. It paused, assessing the situation, green eyed, then it leapt on to the arm of Swayne's chair and a moment or two later it had settled, tail and paws tucked in, tidily disposed for sleep.

Unnecessarily, Wycliffe said: "Your cat?"

Swayne stroked the creature. "Clarence—my family, and a lot less trouble than some other families I could mention.

"Anyway, getting back to the Glynns . . . Shortly after taking over the shop Alfred fell in love with the sort of girl men have fantasies about, and she seemed to respond. Nobody knew much about her, she'd turned up in the town as a sort of companion-housekeeper to an old lady who had a house in Morrab Close, a Mrs. Armitage—a widow. I think she was a relative. Anyway, Alfred couldn't believe his luck; he'd never really made it with girls and here he was hitting the jackpot. The old lady died and within weeks they'd decided to get married; they started furnishing the rooms over the shop and all was set for a wedding."

Swayne paused, watching the smoke curl upwards from his little cigar. "Well there was a wedding all right, but it was Matthew who married the girl."

Wycliffe was roused. "You mean you've been talking about—what was she called?—Inez, the mother of Matthew's children?"

"Exactly, and it didn't improve matters from Alfred's point of view when he discovered that she was already a couple of months pregnant by Matthew when she married him."

"It must have caused a scandal."

"It didn't actually. The Glynns have always played their cards close to their chests and, like Clarence here, they have the knack of fading into the background when it suits them. There was a certain amount of gossip but it soon died down."

Wycliffe was impressed. "And then, eleven years later, she walked out on Matthew and her three children."

Swayne gave a short laugh. "That was Inez—that was!" After a pause he went on: "I think you'll agree that Alfred had good reason to feel aggrieved. From the time of the marriage he cut himself off entirely from his brother, but it wasn't only from Matthew: he became more and more of a recluse until now he hardly sees anyone but the people he meets in the course of his business —and they're getting fewer by the month. Until his mother died he used to pay a routine Wednesday visit but, of course, that's stopped now."

"Do you have any contact with him?"

Swayne smiled. "One of the privileged few. I felt sorry for Alfred at the time—I still do. I look in occasionally for a drink and a chat though he's getting more and more difficult to talk to. As a matter of fact, Matthew asked me to keep an eye on him—I think he felt guilty."

When Swayne stopped speaking small sounds reached them from the street: a woman's heels tapping on the paving stones, a snatch of conversation from the people opposite . . . Swayne waited for some comment on his revelations, a word of commendation, even thanks, but when Wycliffe spoke it was on a quite different subject.

"What happened last night?"

"You mean, what happened here?"

Wycliffe said nothing. There were advantages in failing to define your terms. Precise questions encourage precise answers while vague ones often elicit more information.

Swayne said: "Matt arrived about half-seven and we played chess—just the one game and it was a rout. Matt was off his game. We chatted a bit, had a drink or two, and he left at half-past nine —said he had work to do in his office."

"The two of you were alone?"

"Yes, Mike Doble usually joins us but he's in hospital at the moment for a heart operation."

"Would you say that Glynn was much as usual?"

A pause to consider. "No, he was preoccupied; worried about the business. He's had problems lately: they need working capital and Matt has a dread of, as he put it, 'getting into the hands of the bank.' I don't think it was anything very serious."

Wycliffe stood up. "Well, thank you for your help, Mr. Swayne. I expect I shall be calling on you again."

Swayne escorted him downstairs and, at his own request, Wycliffe left by way of the backyard.

"Is this what Glynn did last night?"

"Yes, he always comes and goes this way."

Some of the backs were dilapidated but the two premises belonging to the Glynns stood out in good repair: the wall had been recently pointed and colour-washed and the door freshly painted.

The door was bolted but Wycliffe banged on it and was admitted by a uniformed policeman.

He could not make up his mind about Swayne. The little man had appeared shocked at the very idea that Alfred might be suspected of killing his brother yet he had gone on, with a certain relish, to provide a convincing motive—if a motive which has lain dormant for thirty years is still convincing. Festering hatred, nurtured and cultivated like a precious plant for half a lifetime, is good stuff for the novelist, but does it happen?

He stood in the middle of the yard. To his right was the single-storey extension which housed Glynn's office with its own exit to the yard. The killer could have reached the office from the lane, or by crossing the yard from the house, or by coming through the shop from the house. The yard door was bolted at 11:15 but a woman—Sara?—was seen to enter by it at around 11:30. Presumably she bolted the door after her for that was how the police had found it in the morning.

There were alternative scenarios: the killer, an outsider, was still with his victim when Gerald tried to get in but, by the time the woman arrived, he had left. Dippy Martin had not seen anyone but he had spent some time at the top of the lane. Alternatively, the killer was someone from the house who had secured the door to ensure privacy, but opened it again after his crime to confirm the impression that an outsider was involved. There were other possibilities but for the moment these seemed the most plausible. Of course it was conceivable that the assailant had climbed the yard wall but, without a ladder of some sort, this would have been an acrobatic feat.

Wycliffe felt like a crossword addict who has some of the clues, a few of the answers but no grid on which to relate them.

The back door of the house opened and a girl came out into the yard. Christine, he supposed, the younger sister. She was shaking a tablecloth when she looked up and saw him. Her expression froze; a vague gesture and she turned to disappear indoors.

Sometimes the strangeness of his job came home to him. What had he to do with that girl? Why should she be troubled by the mere sight of him? A few hours ago he had not known that she existed, now he was a licensed voyeur, authorized to meddle in her most intimate concerns.

In the office Fox and his team had completed their work including an inventory. "Except the safe, sir." Fox had a grievance, his manner was indignant. "I found the key eventually, it was in Glynn's bedroom—in a little bureau drawer with other keys. I asked to have one of the family present when I opened the safe but Gerald objects to it being opened at all without their solicitor being present. That would mean putting it off until tomorrow."

"Well?"

"I told him I would ask you."

"It sounds reasonable, tell him to arrange for his solicitor to be here in the morning."

"But he's being deliberately obstructive."

"Perhaps, but that's life, Fox. Put a seal on the safe and we'll see what's inside in the morning. By the way, have you ever taken a cat's paw-prints?"

Fox was wary. "I can't say I have—a dog's, sir, but never a cat's."

"Have a try with Swayne's cat next door; he might have made the bloody marks on the carpet. His name is Clarence, by the way. Be nice to him—and to Swayne—and find out, if you can, what time Clarence came in last night."

Fox was disapproving. "I take it you are serious, sir?"

"As a judge."

It was late afternoon. That morning Wycliffe had heard of the Glynn family for the first time and in the few hours since he had learned something about them; about Gerald, Gina, and Barry, about Christine and Aunt Sara, and about the uncles, Alfred and Maurice. But he was still a very long way from knowing enough to judge the value of what each of them had chosen, or would choose to tell him, and what they would, for differing reasons, see fit to suppress.

Above all he knew little more about Matthew Glynn than might reasonably appear in his obituary, but he needed to know the man well enough to see him going about his daily life against the background of his home and shop and in the context of his family, friends, and acquaintances.

"Glynn's bedroom—which room is it?"

"Opposite the top of the stairs, sir."

"And the bureau—is it locked?"

"Yes, but the key was among those in Glynn's pocket. I've got them here." Fox handed over the key-fold.

Wycliffe went through the shop and entered the house by the communicating door. It opened into a passage which ran the length of the house. Voices came from somewhere at the back— probably the kitchen: families seem to favour the kitchen as an assembly point in times of crisis. He had intended to visit Matthew's bedroom alone but changed his mind and went to the kitchen. He knocked and opened the door.

They were standing around in frozen postures like a group caught when the music stops in a game of Statues.

"Miss Glynn—Miss Sara Glynn?"

Sara wasn't in the kitchen but a voice behind him said: "You wanted me, Superintendent?" He had not heard her approach.

"I shall be grateful if you will show me your brother's room."

He followed Sara up the stairs and into Matthew's bedroom. The heavy wardrobe, the dressing-table with triple mirrors, the tallboy—all in walnut—and the matching double bed with its honeycomb quilt, belonged to the era of Matthew's father or even his grandfather.

Above the mantelpiece, in a place of honour, was an enlarged photograph of a middle-aged woman with the hairstyle and in the dress of the forties; it was inscribed, boldly: "To Matt, from Mother."

Wycliffe looked at the massive double bed. "Did your brother sleep in this room when your father was alive?"

"No, he moved in here only recently—after Mother died." A curve of the lips. "Of course it was the bedroom belonging to the head of the house but he couldn't have turned Mother out." The irony was bitter.

"I see. I'm sorry to inflict this on you, Miss Glynn, but I want to look at the contents of the bureau amongst other things and it is better that a member of the family should be present. It's also a chance to have another word with you."

His manner was pleasant but she was unresponsive; she stood, motionless in the middle of the room, as though waiting patiently for her services to be called upon.

The bureau which was against the window wall and the chair beside it did not match the rest of the furniture. Wycliffe unlocked and lowered the flap. Everything was in meticulous order: envelopes and headed paper in pigeonholes, a section for unpaid bills, another for receipted accounts; a box for stamps. Evidently Matthew had kept his personal affairs quite separate from his shop and council business.

The bureau had a single, locked drawer and in it, amongst other things, Wycliffe found a cheque book, a paying-in book, and a sheaf of bank statements clipped together. While still leafing through the statements he turned to Sara: "We have a witness who claims to have seen you in Alexandra Road after eleven on Saturday night, and you may know that a woman was seen going in by the back door of this house at half-past."

Wycliffe did not look up from the statements and for some time

Sara gave no sign that she had heard; then she said: "I've been very stupid. One does something on the spur of the moment that is trivial and perhaps a little silly, then when that action is caught up in . . . in a tragic event, one feels quite foolish telling of it."

Wycliffe had transferred his attention from statements to cheque stubs. "So what did you do on Saturday night?"

"As I told you, I spent some time writing letters and when I'd finished I thought it would be pleasant to get some fresh air so I went out and posted them—in the box outside the main post office—"

"What time was that?"

"About a quarter past ten. It was pleasant out-of-doors and I went for a walk, down by the station, along the wharf and across the promenade."

"Surely it was raining?"

"Now and then, but I don't mind the rain."

"You went out and came back by the yard door?"

"Yes."

"And you saw nothing either going or returning to the house which seemed suspicious or even unusual?"

"Nothing."

"Did you enter the house through the kitchen door or through your brother's office and the shop?"

"Why should I go through his office? I saw the light there and assumed that he was working."

Wycliffe said nothing for a while but continued with his study of the cheque stubs. When he spoke it was to change the subject. "Your brother seems to have had little use for credit cards."

She seemed surprised by the new topic, perhaps relieved. At any rate she came to stand by the bureau. "Matthew had very old-fashioned views about credit, even in running the business."

Wycliffe held out a cheque stub folded to expose a particular counterfoil. "A cheque in favour of Eurotravel, dated a couple of weeks ago. Was he planning a trip?"

"Yes, a holiday; he intended to go away in May—it was a regular thing. He had two holidays a year: in May he usually went abroad for a fortnight, then in October he would have another fortnight somewhere in this country."

"Do you know where he intended going next month?"

"He tried to visit a different European country on each of his spring trips." She smiled. "I think it was Bulgaria's turn this year."

"He went on these trips alone?"

"Oh, yes; I often wonder how he managed; he wasn't the sort to make friends easily but he seemed to enjoy himself. Of course they were package tours though he seems to have spent a surprising amount on this one. Matthew was so careful with his money in most things."

A few things remained in the bureau drawer; the odds and ends that accumulate in drawers: an engagement diary for 1981 which had only a few entries; an old wallet, empty except for an out-of-date RAC membership card.

"Your brother seems to have kept nothing to remind him of his wife."

"Does that surprise you? When it was obvious that Inez was not coming back he packed up everything connected with her and stored it in one of the attics. He did it himself. No one was allowed to go through her belongings."

"She was still the mother of his children."

Sara said nothing.

Wycliffe returned everything to the drawer. He was in the act of locking the bureau flap when he said: "Miss Glynn, what made you go into your brother's office this morning when you came down, as you say, to make yourself a cup of tea?"

She was terse. "I told you; I saw the light."

"No."

"I beg your pardon!"

"It was daylight at the time and the curtains in your brother's office were drawn."

It took her a second or two to recover. "But I'm sure I saw a light . . . If the curtains were slightly parted—"

"Were they?"

"I am trying to remember the exact circumstances; I am not accustomed to having my word questioned."

Wycliffe stood looking at her, his face expressionless. She was trying to decide between aggression and a more conciliatory approach but Wycliffe cut her short.

"I advise you to think very carefully about what you have told me, Miss Glynn, and then to volunteer a statement."

When Wycliffe left the Glynn house a bell in the church, almost next door, was tolling for evening service; not the usual tumbling peal but a monotonous counting out of strokes on the tenor bell, presumably in token of respect for bereaved neighbours. He had to make his way past people converging on the church and was pointed out by several.

About half the tables in the hotel dining-room were occupied but Wycliffe, with Kersey and Lucy Lane, was placed in one of the window embrasures, which gave them all the privacy they could have wished.

Detective Sergeant Lucy Lane was an established member of the Serious Crimes Squad and she more than earned her keep. She was also an attractive girl. With her mass of dark hair, her so-called classical features, and a slender body, she might have been a Klimt model clad in sober woollies instead of erotic raiment.

The fact that Wycliffe often deferred to her judgement made Kersey suspicious of her intrusion into their cosy male councils.

The food was good: a thin soup followed by pork spare ribs. A white-haired waiter with a drooping moustache confided that the marinade was a speciality of the chef. They drank Chablis, nicely chilled.

Kersey said: "Worth starving for."

"Let's finish the bottle."

Lucy, with her hand over her glass, said: "No more for me."

With the cheese Wycliffe told them of his interview with Swayne, and of Sara's revised version of her doings the previous evening.

Kersey said: "So Matthew married Alfred's girlfriend after getting her pregnant; not exactly fraternal conduct, but as a motive for murder it's surely worn a bit thin after thirty years."

Wycliffe turned to Lucy: "What did you make of Alfred?"

Lucy patted her lips with her table napkin. "I'm not sure." That in itself was unusual. Lucy rarely prevaricated. "I felt sorry for him. He's living alone in near squalor and he's obviously a sick man."

"You must have got something."

"It was difficult. His sister, Sara, had been to see him and I think she must have upset him. Of course I don't know what he's usually like. I couldn't keep him to any particular point—he kept slipping from one subject to another without seeming to realize it."

Kersey helped himself to a little more of the Stilton. "In other words, he's a bit gaga."

Lucy frowned. "I'm not so sure about that. My impression was that I was only getting a small part of his attention, that he was profoundly preoccupied and that the one thing he wanted was to be left alone."

"Was he afraid?"

"Afraid?" She shook her head. "Certainly not of me or of anything I might do."

"In your opinion, would he have been physically capable of the killing?"

"I think so; after all it wasn't a job for a muscle man. I suppose you knew that he had medical training?"

"He told you that himself?"

"In one of his digressions. He either failed or didn't take his finals; I couldn't make out which."

Kersey said: "I find it hard to believe that anybody, even a nut, would murder after thirty years of procrastination."

Lucy emptied her wine glass. "Perhaps the fact that his mother had only recently died had something to do with it."

Wycliffe nodded. "That's a point we mustn't overlook in all this. What was his attitude to Matthew?"

"It's hard to say. His first comment was: 'I haven't seen much of Matthew recently'—as though they hadn't happened to meet in the street for a week or two—not that they hadn't spoken for nearly thirty years."

"Any particular antagonism?"

"Not obviously. His attitude was that of a well-bred man reluctant to discuss some family difference with a prying outsider. To be honest I couldn't make up my mind about him and I'd like you to see him yourself."

Outside the hotel window people strolled past, trailed by their dogs; Penzance must have a high rating in the doggy charts. Others watched the sea from their parked cars strung out along the promenade. It was a fine evening, the sea was an unruffled expanse of silvery blue; the Mount stood out, a grey-green pyramid with its fairy-tale castle at the top catching the low sun. Everything was in sharp focus, the horizon was a clear line dividing sea and sky; more rain about.

Kersey brushed biscuit crumbs from his jacket. "Coming back to Sara: she went to post a letter, took a little walk in the rain, heard nothing, saw nothing and said nothing about it because she felt silly—is that it, sir?"

"Just about."

"Do you believe it?"

"I've asked her to think over her position, including her story about seeing a light in her brother's office from the kitchen this morning. I've suggested she should volunteer a fresh statement."

Wycliffe folded his table napkin and got up from his chair. "Whatever Sara might or might not have done, I think I'll go for a walk."

It was predictable whenever he was away from home—the stroll before bed—and they both knew better than to offer their company. He walked to Newlyn, where the paintings and the pilchards came from in the old days, and returned along the sea-front with the streetlamps struggling against the great plain of darkness that was the sea. Eventually he went to sleep to the sound of little waves lapping against the sea-wall.

CHAPTER FIVE

Monday morning

The Incident Room premises secured by Shaw were part of a complex of old buildings near the wharf which were suffering from planning blight. If their historical interest had saved them from the pick, the swinging steel ball, and the bulldozer, their intractable layout had discouraged renovators who might have put them to some use. The rooms were over a former shop now used by a small-time printer, and the clacking and rumbling of his press would underscore the activities of the squad.

Already equipment and furniture were being delivered from central stores and technicians were installing a communications unit. The smallest of the three rooms had been set aside for the officer in charge; it had a desk, a couple of chairs, and a telephone which, allegedly, would soon be functional. Wycliffe looked about him and approved, especially of the walls which, in some past time, had been stencilled with designs that were mildly but cheerfully crazy so that to look at them for long made the eyes go funny. Another plus: the window of this room looked out over grey slate roofs to the harbour and Albert Pier.

"Incident Rooms I have Known": Wycliffe could have written a book about them.

At the briefing he agreed to see Alfred, while Kersey would talk to the son-in-law, Barry Morse. "The outsider," Wycliffe called him. "Gossip has it that he's a good accountant, keen on music, and henpecked. I don't suppose the three are incompatible but that's all we know about him. Among other things you might get his view of the bookshop and of his father-in-law as a businessman."

Kersey grumbled: "I don't go down well with bank managers, accountants, and others of the breed; we are *non simpatico*. Why not let Shaw do it?"

Wycliffe was brusque. "Because Shaw has his hands full with the Incident Room and you've got the rank. When you've finished with Morse see what you can find out about Inez Glynn's disappearance; the records should be available by now.

"Incidentally, when Inez went, Matthew collected all her belongings together, everything that reminded him of her, and stored them in one of the attics; nobody else was allowed to touch the stuff. I'm arranging for Fox to go through it."

"You think there's a connection?"

"I've no idea."

Lucy Lane was assigned to the bookshop; among other things to keep an eye on the opening of the safe. House-to-house enquiries would continue with special attention to Matthew's acquaintances in business and in his council activities.

A steep alley provided a shortcut from the wharf area to Lady Street. The street looked very different from its Sunday image; the shops were open and delivery vans effectively blocked the way for all but the most resolute pedestrians. It had rained overnight but now the sun was breaking through and the scene had a certain gaiety. Seagulls swooped and planed overhead laying raucous claim to some scrap of food in the possession of one of them. It was nine by the church clock and another clock over a bank in the town hammered out the strokes.

"Alfred Glynn, MPS. Chemist and Druggist." The sign, in faded letters, was suspended over a shop window cluttered with a dusty, neglected display of sickroom adjuncts and toilet articles along with dummy boxes and bottles and tins advertising baby foods and patent medicines. There were two or three granite steps up to the front door which had a grubby Closed notice hung behind its glass panel; no bell, and no other door. Wycliffe decided to approach from the rear. He had to go through the churchyard to reach the back lane so he counted the houses to be sure of identifying Alfred's door. It was devoid of paint and dragged on its hinges. Part of the yard was taken up with a shed, the rest was a wilderness of weed with a slate path up to the back door.

He walked up the path. There was a bell-push by the door and he pressed it. A bell sounded somewhere in the house but there was no response. After two more attempts he tried the door; it was unsecured and it opened into a little hall from which stairs led upwards.

He called: "Mr. Glynn!"

Still no answer. After a short wait he climbed the stairs and at the top he called again. The only sound came from the ticking of a clock. Several doors opened off the landing and there were ladder-like stairs which presumably led to the attics. He tried the first door, it opened into the kitchen; the second led to the living-room. He called once more without result then advanced into the room. It was L-shaped and only when he reached the corner of the "L" could he see the whole of the room. There was no one there.

It was a cheerless, comfortless room; only tattered books on makeshift shelves and an old-fashioned record player suggested any kind of relaxation; no radio, no television. There were no pictures on the walls but on the mantelpiece, amongst a random collection of odds and ends, there was a framed photograph of an elderly woman; her hair was gathered into an old-fashioned bun on the top of her head; she had a smooth, rather spoilt face and an expression of absolute serenity. The photograph was inscribed: "To Alfred from Mother, at 75."

A single-bar electric fire stood in front of the empty grate and a wing-backed chair, threadbare and with broken springs, was drawn up in front of it. On a low table by the chair were the remnants of a spartan breakfast—a few crumbs of toast, a tub of margarine, and a mug with coffee dregs at the bottom; also a book, open but face down: Le Carré's *The Honourable Schoolboy*.

Morning light streamed through the window searching out the shabbiness and the dust, the peeling walls and cobwebbed corners. Through the window he could see over grey slate roofs across the bay to Newlyn, a mound of little houses behind its quays and boats and sheds. A shaft of sunlight caught the hill above the village turning the fields acid green.

Wycliffe returned to the landing and tried another door: the bathroom and lavatory. The Victorian stoneware "suite" from Mr. Twyford's manufactory was decorated with flowers in willow-

pattern blue but paint flaked off the walls and the linoleum had
worn through to the floorboards. The next room was Alfred's
bedroom: an iron bedstead with a tumbled mass of greyish bed-
ding, a chest of drawers and a non-matching wardrobe. There
were more books in a nest of shelves by the bed.

For no reason he could think of the rooms reminded him of a
deserted stage set when the play has ended its run and the actors
have gone.

But it was the main bedroom which came as a surprise and a
shock.

The room was in the front of the house and the window overlooking the narrow street was hung with net curtains and pale
blue velvet drapes which were almost completely drawn. It was a
moment before his eyes became accustomed to the gloom.

The room had been vandalized—viciously so; but it was equally
apparent that it had been furnished and cared for at a level totally
different from the other rooms. The double bed, the wardrobe,
dressing-table, and tallboy were mahogany, the counterpane was
of moire silk and the eiderdown was covered in the same material;
the carpet was a red-ground Wilton. But the polished surfaces of
the furniture had been scored, even gouged; the counterpane had
been cut to ribbons and the eiderdown slit open in several places.
A carriage clock lay smashed on the floor beside an art-nouveau
lamp; and the bedside table on which, presumably, they had both
stood, had been split almost in two.

On the carpet by the tallboy were several red carnations, as
fresh as they had come from the florist, and beside them, a shattered glass spill. Water from the spill had soaked the carpet. Also
on the floor were three or four framed pictures which had been
trampled—stamped upon, so that the frames were broken and the
glass shattered to fragments. They were photographic enlarge-
ments, head-and-shoulders portraits, all of the same girl, photo-
graphed in profile; looking up and looking down, and seen from
the right and from the left.

So this was Inez, the *femme fatale* of the Glynn brothers: her
features were patrician: a long, slender neck, pouting, sensuous
lips, a slightly aquiline nose, and sloping forehead—a model for an
Egyptian tomb-painting or limestone relief. This was Inez in her

early twenties, before she became the mother of Matthew's children. In the mingling of the genes the children had missed their mother's sculptural beauty and been forced to settle for mere good looks.

The double bed had been made up for two and there were two pyjama cases—relics of a past time—one embroidered with the letter *I,* the other with an *A.* But it was obvious that the room was never used; it was a museum, perhaps a shrine. So, for thirty years Alfred Glynn had preserved this room as it had been when he still believed that the silk counterpane and the eiderdown would be the covers on his marriage bed. He had not only preserved the room, he had cleaned it with meticulous care and provided fresh flowers in the little glass spill. Here was the connubial complement to Miss Havisham's wedding feast but without the cobwebs.

Now, certainly within the last twenty-four hours, the room had been vandalized.

By Alfred himself? Or by another? And where was Alfred?

He did not remember having seen a telephone. He returned to the living-room and found that what he had taken to be a cupboard door, in fact gave access by a flight of stairs to the shop. As he descended he was aware of a distinctive blend of smells recalling chemist shops of his childhood; it was compounded of, among other things, disinfectant, Parma violets, and balsam. The shop was dimly lit and cluttered but he found his way to the front door which was bolted; Alfred had not left and could not return that way.

At the other end of the shop, behind a hammered-glass screen, was the dispensary and, adjoining that, a tiny office—with a telephone. He tried the number of the Incident Room, found that it was functional, and spoke to the duty officer.

"I'm at the pharmacy. I want DS Fox here with his team and a uniformed man. They should come by the back door. Is Mr. Kersey or DS Lane there?"

"No, sir, but DS Shaw is."

"Then ask him to come to the phone."

Shaw spent most of his time on organization and records; he was rarely involved directly in enquiries but he had been a first-class man on the ground.

"Shaw speaking, sir."

"I want you to organize enquiries as to the whereabouts of Alfred Glynn, starting at the bookshop then going on to residents in the street who might have seen him; get in touch with his brother at the pottery. No alarm as yet; it's quite possible that he's gone for one of his walks or he may be shopping or just visiting someone, but I'm concerned."

While phoning, Wycliffe opened drawers and cupboards in the Dickensian desk at which he was standing. One cupboard was stacked with old prescription books while one of the drawers held enough sealing wax to supply a pre-war dispensary with red seals on the drug packets of a generation.

He was momentarily startled by the ringing of a doorbell. He had to climb the stairs to the living-room then go down again to the back door. They had sent him a WPC who looked like a schoolgirl dressed in police uniform for a school play.

"WPC Ferrers, sir. DS Fox is on his way."

"Do you know Alfred Glynn?"

"Yes, sir, I've lived here all my life."

"I want you to stay here in the yard until he returns. When he does—if he does—report to DS Fox before you let Glynn into the house, and leave the explanations to Fox."

"What about the front of the premises, sir?"

Young she might be, stupid she was not. "The shop door is bolted on the inside so he can't get in that way."

Fox arrived with an assistant and Wycliffe took him to the vandalized room. "It's obvious that this is all fresh, probably done this morning. I want to know whether it was done by Glynn himself or by an outsider. Glynn's prints must be all over the premises so there should be no problem."

"Are we authorized to be here, sir?"

"No, but that is my responsibility. If Glynn turns up you will be warned by the WPC. Go easy on him; one way or another he is or will be very distressed."

Wycliffe left the house feeling disoriented as he did when emerging from the darkness and isolation of a cinema into reality and the light of day. Lady Street had returned to what must have been normal for any morning at this time; the delivery vans had gone, there was sporadic traffic in the one-way street, and people had no time to stand about gawping at the bookshop though they slowed their pace in passing and tried to look in without appearing to do so. There was a notice on the door: "Closed temporarily; all enquiries by telephone please."

Wycliffe turned down the alley towards the Incident Room. The printer, running off posters on his flat-bed press, was going through operations not significantly different from those performed by Caxton five hundred years earlier. Police vehicles were tucked into every available space in the crooked, meandering alley and police personnel, uniformed and CID, were continually clattering up and down the stairs which led to the room above the printer's. An alien presence had established itself in the heart of the town and people who had no connection with the crime under investigation or any other would feel uneasy until they were gone.

"Paula!" Sara was brusque. "You were in and out of this office all the time, you must have some idea of what my brother kept in his safe."

Paula James, Matthew Glynn's youthful amanuensis (after a one-year course in office routines at the technical college) had turned up for work as usual, unaware of the events which had robbed her of her employer. She found herself in his office, the centre of a family gathering with their lawyer and a policewoman. Slightly confused, but by no means intimidated, she assumed an air of aggressive detachment.

"What was in the safe, Miss Glynn, was nothing to do with me. I only saw it open a few times but as far as I remember there were a couple of old ledgers and a stack of pocket files."

They were all there except Christine, even Barry Morse, who must have taken time off from his job, presumably to lend support to his wife and the family. The presence of the lawyer contributed to the melodrama of the situation. Grouped around the safe, against the light, almost in silhouette, they were a study for a Victorian painter, ready-made for his party piece at the RA Summer Exhibition—*The Safe*.

Gerald was impatient. "Let's get on with it!" He turned to Lucy Lane: "Are you going to break those seals?"

Lucy looked at the lawyer, who nodded. She broke the seals, inserted a key, turned it, twisted the brass handle, and opened the heavy door. At first sight it was as Paula had said: two ledger-like volumes, quite thick, bound in worn red leather and lettered on their spines in faded gilt. These were on the shelf and the bottom of the safe was stacked with pocket files. At the top a metal drawer extended the whole width.

"Well, let's see what's in there, Gina!"

Gina looked at her brother, about to say something cutting but changed her mind. She lifted out the books; they were quarto, half-bound in leather, and heavy. She held the faded spine of one of them to the light so that she could read the lettering: "Journal of Martin J. Beale 1852–67." The other was dated 1868–84. The books were in manuscript and the text was interspersed with lively pen-and-ink sketches.

Jordan, the lawyer—a tubby little man, very dark, with glasses which made him look owlish—said: "Do you know anything about these books, Gina?"

"I've never seen them before."

Sara said: "But rare books are your department."

Gina turned on her aunt in irritation: "I tell you I've never seen them before and I've no idea where they came from."

Gina had the first volume open at the initial entry and she read aloud: " 'Durban, Natal, Thursday, January 1st, 1852. It occurs to me, being in this place at this time with no sign of an approaching end to the Kaffir war and all things uncertain, that it may be of interest to record the passages of everyday life if only as a source of remembrance and reflection in later years. I am twenty-six years old . . .' "

Gina turned the pages of the other volume. "The whole journal appears to have been written in South Africa but he moved to Cape Province, and from later entries it seems he was in contact with Cecil Rhodes . . ."

The lawyer said: "Are the books valuable?"

Gina swept the hair from her eyes in a characteristic gesture. "I suppose they must be, as historical documents in their own right, and as material for a publisher. I should have to get other opinions but I'd guess they would fetch a good deal of money at auction. I just don't understand where Father got them or why he kept them hidden like this."

The lawyer was cautious: "I wouldn't say they were hidden, Gina. In any case, can we get on?"

Lucy Lane interrupted, authority in her voice: "Before we move on, others of you must have seen the safe open from time to time; it would be useful if we could establish how long the books have been there."

Sara said: "I can't see what possible connection these books could have with my brother's death."

"Perhaps there is none but it is a possibility, however remote."

There was a brief silence, then Gerald spoke up: "I've seen the safe open several times since I've been working in the business. The books have always been there as far as I can remember. Like Paula, I thought they were old ledgers and I didn't take much notice. In any case the old man wasn't the sort to let you take a close look at anything that didn't directly concern you."

"Miss Glynn?" Suddenly they were being interrogated.

Sara made an effort to appear offhand. "I'm not often in here. I suppose I've seen Matthew with the safe open, and I may have noticed the books, but this firm has been going for more than a century and one doesn't take much notice of such things, one has grown up with them."

"Mr. Morse?"

Barry seemed more ill at ease than the others. "As you know I don't work in the firm but I do give a hand with the accounts from time to time—"

"You work in here on those occasions?"

"Yes, I do, but I don't think I've ever seen the safe open." A nervous smile. "It is almost axiomatic in businesses like this that nothing of value is ever kept in the safe."

Lucy said: "That, apparently, wasn't the case here."

"No . . . No, indeed!"

The pocket files were lifted out. All of them contained agendas and minutes of council committee meetings. The metal drawer was opened and found to be empty. There remained only a cardboard box lodged behind where the journals had been.

Lucy Lane said: "What's in the box?"

Gina lifted it out. "It's empty." It was rectangular and it had a lid, like a shoe box, but it was longer. The ornately printed label on one end read: "Hatchard's Patent Stencils: This box contains all the materials and instructions necessary to become proficient in the art of stencilling." Gina said: "It's Victorian."

The box was not quite empty, it contained a tiny linen bag tied with a gilt cord and with a lavender head embroidered on it.

Gerald was impatient: "Do we have to waste time on an empty box?"

Lucy Lane said: "People don't usually put empty boxes into a safe. One wonders what was in it. Does anybody know?"

It appeared that no one did.

Kersey was waiting for Morse when he left the safe party. "Detective Inspector Kersey; a word, Mr. Morse . . ."

Morse looked at his watch. "I want to put in an appearance at the office before lunch."

"I'll keep you no longer than necessary."

The others had left. Lucy Lane looked at Kersey. "Will you need me, sir?"

"I think we shall manage."

Back in Matthew Glynn's office, Kersey seated himself in the swivel chair behind the desk and casually waved Morse to a client's chair on the other side. Morse hesitated then decided there was no alternative to sitting down. Kersey lit a cigarette; before uttering a word he was finding out how the accountant reacted to boorish police tactics. The answer was with dignified resignation.

"Profitable morning, Mr. Morse?"

Morse was in good shape physically, slender though muscular, even athletic, but the blond hair, the almost girlish colouring, and the Rupert Brooke profile, held no appeal for Kersey who had a face like a sad clown and the physique of a youngish gorilla.

Morse took his time to answer: "In what way might it have been profitable?"

"A will? Isn't that what families look for in safes—especially when they invite a lawyer to see fair play. Of course I could be wrong; I'm not well up in these things."

Morse subjected him to a long unblinking stare before saying:

"There was no will in the safe and, according to the lawyer, it is unlikely that my father-in-law made one."

"Awkward for you all." Kersey adopted a confidential manner. "As a matter of fact it was about your father-in-law's business affairs that I wanted to talk to you. You realize, of course, that we have to go into these things—no details at this stage; we can get them later from his bank and his lawyer; just the overall picture. It seemed best to have a friendly chat with one of the family not, perhaps, so emotionally involved—and you being an accountant . . ."

Morse was cool. "If you ask me what you want to know I'll see if I can tell you."

Kersey blew out a great cloud of grey smoke. "Good! The bookshop—prosperous? Doing well?"

Morse considered. "I can see that such questions could seem relevant to your enquiry and for that reason I'm prepared to be frank. The business is not going well though sales are good—higher than one might expect in a town of this size and against significant competition—"

"What's wrong then?"

"Overheads are too high and too much money is tied up in slow-moving stock. On any reasonable system of accounting, the second-hand and rare book departments are losing money and are heavily in debt to the other side of the business—"

"So what—"

But Morse would not be interrupted. "My father-in-law was well aware of all this; it has been going on for some years but he would not do what was necessary to right the situation, that is cut out the loss makers and, perhaps, substitute other lines—stationery, office equipment, videos or any other line compatible with the book trade."

"So what did he do?"

"He realized on other assets and used the money to subsidize the business."

"A short-term policy, surely?"

A thin smile. "My father-in-law was giving new meaning to the phrase 'keeping a shop.' "

"Does all this account for the proposed development at the pottery?"

"I suppose so."

"A last resort?"

Morse hesitated. "I had thought so but recently he hinted at another asset he hoped to dispose of that would bring in quite a lot of money. He did not say what it was but it may be that we found it in the safe this morning. Your sergeant will tell you about that." Morse looked at his watch and stood up. "Now, if you will excuse me, I really should—"

"Just one more question. Do other members of the family agree with your diagnosis and your proposed remedy?"

"Gerald does—decisively; my wife too, but she is swayed by loyalty to her father."

"And Sara?"

"Sara has never concerned herself with the business."

Kersey watched him go, an appreciative grin on his face. Full marks for presentation and content. Barry was by no means negligible.

Wycliffe was back in the Incident Room. "Any news of Alfred Glynn?"

The duty officer was DC Holman, a local man, young enough to be ambitious and anxious to make the most of this chance to work with the crime squad.

"They knew nothing at the bookshop, sir; his sister, Sara, seemed very upset; she wouldn't believe that he wasn't at home. I think she's gone down there. Anyway, there's been a report from a chambermaid at the hotel; she says she saw Alfred just before eight this morning, on his way up the street. According to her he looked ill; she spoke to him but he didn't seem to see her."

In the little office set aside for him, Wycliffe brooded over the accumulating mound of paper, the expanding case file, and among the rest a preliminary report from Franks on the autopsy. It told him nothing new. Matthew Glynn had become a subject: "Caucasian male, aged fifty-two . . . No observable lesions other than those arising from the assault . . . Death due to anoxia resulting from strangulation . . ."

And there was a memo from Fox: "Re cat, property of Ronald Swayne of 22a, Lady Street. Casts of the paw-prints of this creature were found to correspond with blooded prints at the scene of crime. Questioned, Swayne stated that the animal had been let out at approximately 9:30 on Saturday evening and was crying to be let in at a little before midnight. According to Swayne, it is the creature's habit to be out for no more than half an hour at night."

Fox on the ethology of *Felis catus.* Wycliffe suspected that the encounter between Fox and Clarence had not been a meeting of kindred souls. Interesting all the same. Somebody must have let the cat out of Glynn's office shortly before midnight and, from Dippy Martin's evidence, the likelihood was that the somebody was a woman.

Wycliffe went to the window and stood looking out over the roof tops to the harbour and Albert Pier. The sun was shining but there was a bank of cloud out to sea; no discernible movement anywhere. Three men stood motionless on the distant pier, part of a great stillness with no other living thing in sight.

Since childhood Wycliffe had experienced episodes when he seemed to see the world about him through fresh eyes, as though, without warning, he had become an intruder in some foreign place, and he would be overcome by the strangeness of it all. There was nothing analytical in the experience, only a sense of wonder that things should be as he saw them and, in particular, that he should be involved.

Now somebody had strangled a fifty-two-year-old man called Matthew Glynn and he was expected to identify and apprehend the killer. Men and women were busy under his supervision investigating and reporting on the lives of people who might or might not have been concerned in the death of this man. But at this moment it was as though he were watching a play . . .

Those three men on the pier, did they too sometimes ask themselves—?

There was a tap at the door and Lucy Lane came in. "Am I disturbing you, sir?"

He motioned her to a chair and sat down himself.

Was she looking at him oddly? Perhaps to keep herself in countenance she opened her notebook although he knew that she would not refer to it.

"A couple of things, sir; I'm not sure whether either of them is relevant. First, Matthew's secretary, the girl who works in the office next door, turned up for work as usual this morning: she lives a few miles out and she knew nothing of what had happened."

"You got something from her?"

"I had a word with her after the safe business was over. She seems a bit spiteful and not very bright but what she had to say was factual."

Lucy Lane was a daughter of the Manse, her father was a very orthodox Methodist parson and Lucy herself was emphatically committed to the side of the angels, often to those with a partiality for flaming swords. Any smoothy who saw her as a soft touch was in for a shock.

She frowned and pushed her notebook aside. "According to her, about a week ago, in his office, Matthew had a row with his brother—"

"With Alfred?"

"With Maurice. There were customers in the shop and even they could hear it."

"We know about that; it seems to have been almost common gossip. Did the girl know what it was about?"

"She knew that it was connected with Matthew wanting to build houses on land adjoining Maurice's pottery. It was the day after the council had agreed to a site meeting to discuss the scheme."

"Anyway I'll be seeing Maurice this afternoon." Wycliffe was returning to earth. "Now, what about the safe opening? Who was there?"

"All of them with the exception of Christine."

Lucy Lane told him about the journal.

"Where are the books now?"

"Back in the safe and I've got the key for the moment. What do you want me to do?"

"Do you have any ideas about them?"

"Not really. Gina thought they must be valuable and she's

probably right; but she's puzzled as to why her father kept them shut away and never mentioned them."

"You think they are involved in some under-the-counter deal?"

"It looks that way."

"Anything else in the safe?"

"Nothing of interest. The lawyer was hoping to find a will but it begins to look as though Matthew died intestate."

"That must have caused a flutter."

"It did." She was still preoccupied.

"Something else on your mind?"

"A small thing, sir. I said there was nothing else in the safe but behind the books there was a cardboard box—rectangular, like a shoe box, but longer."

"What was in it?"

"Nothing; at least only a lavender sachet."

"So?"

"You don't put an empty box in a safe; there must have been something in it when it was put there and the lavender sachet makes me think it must have been something of sentimental value."

"That sounds reasonable."

She grinned. "It sounds stupid, but I can't help associating the box with the journal—"

They were interrupted by the arrival of Kersey. He came in looking sour as he usually did when he found Wycliffe conferring with Lucy Lane. "They told me you were here, sir . . . If I'm not interrupting . . ."

He hooked one of the bentwood chairs into position with his foot and sat on it astride, arms resting on the back.

Wycliffe said: "You've heard that Alfred seems to have taken himself off?"

"After wrecking the place—yes."

"As to who did the wrecking, we have to wait to hear from Fox, but I've got a search organized for Alfred. Anyway, did you talk to Morse?"

Kersey felt in his pockets for his cigarettes. "Yes, he isn't a bad bloke actually; almost human. He says the bookshop is in trouble."

"Financially?"

"It seems that Matthew was running the thing on too big a scale for the size of the town—too much stock of the wrong sort and overheads too high." Kersey lit a cigarette and with a wry grin enquired: "Am I being antisocial?" He was thawing.

"Yes, but we'll live with it. What more did you get?"

"Matthew has been realizing on other assets to keep the business afloat. Morse said it lent a new meaning to the phrase 'keeping a shop.' "

"And the next step was to build houses around his brother's pottery."

Kersey nodded. "So it seems."

Lucy Lane said: "I wonder he didn't cash in on the journal."

Which involved an explanation to Kersey.

At the end of it Kersey said: "That figures. Morse seemed to think you'd found something in the safe which Matthew regarded as a negotiable asset."

Wycliffe was impatient. "This is all very well but I don't see in any of it a motive for murder. I know that many killings are done for next to nothing but we are not dealing with street muggers or footloose louts, we are dealing with the middle-aged and the middle-class—people who know which side their bread is buttered and value their reputations almost more than their deeds and their share certificates. In my experience fear is the most powerful drive to violence among such people and why should any of them in this case be afraid?"

CHAPTER SIX

Monday afternoon

Wycliffe was on his way to St. Hilary, to the Trebyan pottery, and Maurice Glynn. There had been no further news of Alfred since he was seen by one of the hotel staff in Lady Street at eight that morning. Fox had completed his examination of the vandalized room and his report was conclusive: no prints, fresh or otherwise, of anyone other than Alfred himself. What was more, Fox was satisfied that the presence of Alfred's fresh prints on the damaged articles was convincing evidence that it was he who had carried out the destruction.

It was very strange.

St. Hilary Churchtown is a small cluster of old, grey-green houses built around the church at a kink in a tree-lined lane. Wycliffe thought that time had passed the place by, that history must have piled day upon day, year upon year, in peace and quietude. He was wrong. In 1932 it had captured international headlines when the church was attacked by a mob of evangelical bigots who went to work with sledgehammers, wrecking altars and destroying ornaments of which they disapproved; perhaps the last violent twitch of the Puritan tail on English soil.

Wycliffe was alone and he had to get out of the car to rouse a sleeping dog in the roadway. A woman was coming towards him, grey haired, plump and freckled; Wycliffe asked her how to get to Trebyan.

"You just keep on for half a mile or so and 'tis up on your left. Are you police? . . . I wondered." She put a freckled, multiringed hand on the car door, effectively barring him from getting back in. " 'Tis a sad thing about poor Matthew and no mistake! But they brothers never had much luck."

She broke off to acknowledge an old man trudging by: "Good day to you, Mr. Ivey! Nice afternoon for a bit of a walk but don't you go overdoing it." She followed the old man with her eyes. "He's gone downhill, lately, poor old chap, but we all got to come to it.

"Anyway, I was saying about the Glynns: Maurice lost his wife when she was no more 'n a girl; Matthew's missus walked out an' left him with three children. Then there's Alfred—I mean, he never had what you'd call a proper life . . ."

She ran on, her voice as smooth and rich as cream.

Wycliffe said: "You obviously know the family."

"My dear life, I should do! They three boys—and Sara—was all brought up at Trebyan and they was all at the village school. 'Course they went on to grammar school as 'twas in they days. But they was living at Trebyan up to when Matthew got married; then their father took that house in P'nzance next to the shop. After they went, Trebyan was let for a year or two till Maurice got hisself married to some up-country girl. Pretty li'l thing she was, but delicate; you could see she wouldn' be long for this world—and they started that pottery thing . . ."

She seemed content to gossip indefinitely but Wycliffe showed no sign of impatience.

"O'course 'tis none o' my business but you won't find Maurice if it's him you want to see; he went off in his li'l truck when we was sitting down to our dinners. But Alfred must be still there."

"Alfred is at Trebyan?"

It was plain that this was the pearl in her oyster.

"Since this morning. I seen him go past about nine an' I hardly knew him! I heard he was changed but my dear life, he's an old man!"

"He was on foot?"

"When I saw him, but he must've come on the bus—it d' stop at the turn an' 'twas about the time. Anyway he never walked from P'nzance, not like he was. I'll swear t' that."

"Well, thank you, Mrs. . . ."

She removed her hand from the car door; the climax had been achieved. "Pascoe—Emily Pascoe. You're welcome."

Wycliffe got back into his car. Odd about Alfred. They had enquired if he was at the pottery and been told that he was not.

Trebyan was a house and a group of former farm buildings on rising ground, adjacent to an area of gorse and hawthorn scrub, both in flower.

There was a farm gate painted white, standing open, and a sign: "Trebyan Pottery: Visitors Welcome."

Wycliffe hoped that he would be.

He drove up a gravelled track past a couple of tethered goats browsing in the hedges. The house was four-square, with a grey-slated hipped roof, overhanging eaves, and a chimney at each end —the archetypal house which children draw. Hanging by the front door was a brass bell with a cord attached to its clapper and a little notice: "Please ring." Wycliffe rang with timidity; even so the silence he had scarcely noticed until now was brutally shattered. But no one came.

He was in what was once the farmyard, now largely grown over; hens pecked amongst the weedy cobbles. To the right there were farm buildings which had been refurbished and through the open door of one of them he could glimpse open shelving displaying rows of pots. Over that door there was a notice: "Retail Shop." To his left the gorse and hawthorn sprawled over the hillside against a backdrop of little Cornish fields disposed in their unique version of three-dimensional geometry.

He was reminded of his childhood and of his father's farm; they too had kept a couple of goats.

He walked over to the shop but it was unattended. He tried other doors: one opened into a former barn, now a workshop. There were two power-driven pottery wheels, plastic bins for clay and slip, and an electric kiln at one end. A glass bull's eye on a switch-panel by the kiln glowed red; the kiln was being fired.

On shelves around the walls there were pots, vases, jugs, pitchers and plaques of all sorts and sizes, leather hard or biscuit fired. But the place was deserted.

He was getting that *Mary Celeste* feeling.

He found a clay store and a packing shed where, along with a mound of straw and some stout boxes, there were a couple of bicycles. He came at last to a small, lean-to workshop where a girl, seated at a bench with her back to him, was decorating a pot placed on a turntable. On her left a group of similar pots awaited attention; others, to her right, had already received the treatment, a vaguely Oriental squiggle to set buyers thinking of Leach and Hamada.

The girl must have heard him but she gave no sign.

He said: "Christine, isn't it? I didn't expect to find you here."

It was still a moment or two before she completed her work on the pot and turned round. "I come here in my spare time."

"You must have heard the bell."

She said nothing.

"Where is Mr. Glynn?"

"He's gone into Penzance to see the family."

"When are you expecting him back?"

She glanced at her watch. "Any time now."

"So you are here on your own?"

"David is over in the field, hoeing potatoes."

Her manner was unresponsive, even sullen.

"Can you leave what you are doing for a while?"

"I suppose so." She cleaned the brush she was using then washed her hands at the sink. She wore bib-and-brace overalls which left her arms bare; the mass of her dark hair accentuated her pallor and she looked drawn, weary, and vulnerable.

"How long have you been here?"

Her responses were slow as though it required an effort to reply. "I came over this morning just after ten."

"Have you seen your Uncle Alfred?"

"No, they phoned to know if he was here."

"You are quite sure that your Uncle Alfred has not been here today?"

She frowned. "I haven't seen him."

"How did you get here?"

"Bicycle."

"Your Uncle Maurice has been gone a couple of hours?"

"About that."

"You saw him go?"

"Yes."

"Was he alone?"

"Yes."

"Was he carrying anything—in the truck, I mean?"

"No."

"I'll be back in a moment."

He went to his car and spoke to the Incident Room on the telephone. "Regarding Alfred Glynn, I want you to get together a small team, with a dog handler, to await instructions. Also to arrange a check on the buses which serve St. Hilary. Was Alfred Glynn on a bus which arrived here at around nine this morning? . . . I shall be in touch again shortly."

Christine was standing where he had left her. "You didn't stay for the safe opening this morning, then?"

"It was nothing to do with me."

He wanted her to talk but he wasn't being very successful, her answers were as near monosyllabic as she could make them. Well, if that was how she wanted it . . . "At what time did you get home on Saturday evening?"

"At half-past ten."

"You had been to a play with David?"

"Yes."

"How did he get home?"

"Bicycle."

When a car engine sounded in the distance, she said with evident relief: "That will be Uncle, I expect."

They moved outside and saw a Land Rover pick-up emerge from the trees. It turned in at the gate and came chuntering up the track to pull up beside them. A middle-aged man, loose limbed and lean, got out of the driving seat and slammed the door. He wore a washed-out denim jacket, jeans, and trainers; his dark hair was beginning to grey.

"Police?"

"Chief Superintendent Wycliffe."

Glynn nodded. "I've been to see the family; I've kept away until now . . . Of course we've been in touch by phone but I wanted to see how things were . . . Come up to the house."

"A moment, Mr. Glynn! Have you seen your brother Alfred this morning?"

"No, I haven't, we're worried about him; but you know that."

"Your brother was seen passing through the village, apparently on his way here, at nine this morning."

Maurice stood still, looking at Wycliffe, incredulous. "But I was here all the morning. You haven't seen him, have you, Chris?"

"I've told him."

Maurice seemed genuinely perplexed. "I don't understand it, he hasn't been here in ten years! Where's David?"

Christine said: "Up in the garden field."

Maurice turned back to Wycliffe. "I don't understand it . . ."

Wycliffe said: "When did you last see your brother, Mr. Glynn?"

"Alfred?" He ran a hand through his wiry hair. "I don't know; I drop in now and then when I'm in town—a fortnight? three weeks, perhaps."

"And your other brother, Matthew?"

"Matt and I had a bust-up in his office a week or so ago. I dare say you've heard about it."

"And that was the last time you saw him?"

"It was. There was no more we could say to each other except through the damned lawyers." He broke off and seemed to hesitate.

"Something on your mind?"

He was reluctant but it came in the end: "I've been thinking; if Alfie really was coming here it's possible he would have taken the shortcut like we did when we were boys. There's a footpath from the road up through the scrub that cuts off two sides of a triangle . . ."

Wycliffe said: "We'd better find out."

He moved off and looked to Maurice to follow.

"You want me to come with you?" He was oddly tense.

"Please."

"I don't even know if it's passable—the gorse . . ."

"We shall soon see."

The two men set off down a narrow path which traversed the slope diagonally. The path was in good shape but occasionally they had to push aside thrusting shoots. Then they came upon a

clearing where there was a hut made of lap-boarding, with a verandah, and built up on bricks.

Maurice was going to continue along the path but Wycliffe
stopped him. "What is this place?"

"Originally my grandmother had it built as a sort of studio . . .
We children used to camp out here in the summer . . ." He
stood, looking up at the little building, feeling constrained to say
more. "This is the first time I've been down here since God knows
when. It's worn well; David must be looking after it with a coat of
stop-rot now and then." He was uneasy, talking to cover his ner-
vousness.

Wycliffe went up the steps to the verandah and peered through
the window, but because of reflections it was not easy to see inside.
The hut appeared to consist of one large room; there was a sink at
one end and an oil stove; a lamp was suspended on gimbals from
the roof. He could see a table and chairs and what seemed to be
the end of a large settee.

Maurice remained standing in the clearing as though anxious to
get on but Wycliffe went along the verandah to the door.

"It will be locked," Maurice said. "I think David will have the
key; he'll show it you if you want to see it."

But the door was not locked and Wycliffe went in.

The settee he had seen from the window was against one wall
and Alfred Glynn was lying on the floor in front of it, his body
oddly contorted.

Wycliffe had never seen Alfred before but he was in no doubt,
the Glynn features and physique were unmistakable. He knelt
down in the constricted space. Even in the dim light he could see
that the face was cyanosed, deeply discoloured, and there were
reddish spots or petechiae in the region of the eyes.

Alfred Glynn was dead.

Maurice was now standing outside the door with his back to the
room; one hand rested on the verandah rail and without turning
round he said: "Is he dead?"

"I'm afraid so."

In a muffled voice Maurice asked: "How did it happen?"

"I don't know." Then: "If you would just confirm that it is your
brother . . ."

Maurice came a little way into the room, looked down at the body and moved away again. A whispered "Yes," and he was back on the verandah, supporting himself on the rail, and bending over as though at any moment he might vomit.

Wycliffe was angry with himself. He had come alone deliberately in the hope that he might get farther with Maurice Glynn by keeping the interview in a low key. Now he had fallen into a trap which the greenest copper would have avoided. He was out of radio contact and faced with the alternatives of returning to the car with Glynn, leaving the body, or sending Glynn alone to telephone.

He joined Maurice outside. "I want you to go back to the house and telephone the Incident Room. Tell the officer what has happened and that I'm here. The first priority is a doctor, but the officer will know what to do. I'll write the number down." He did so and handed the slip of paper to Maurice.

Maurice took it without a word and, after a moment, shambled off up the path by which they had come.

There would be broad grins in the Incident Room. "The Old Man trod in it this time!"

Wycliffe turned back to the dead man. He looked at his watch. "At approximately 1525, in company with Maurice Glynn, I discovered the body of the deceased lying in a contorted position . . ." It was unusual for a chief super to have to give evidence of the discovery of a body.

Despite the mildness of the day Alfred was wearing a black overcoat over a dark suit which included a waistcoat and there was a homburg hat on the settee. All were so shabby they might have been worn by a dressy tramp. There had been a struggle, buttons had been ripped from the waistcoat, which was open, and a silver pocket watch dangled from its silver chain. Alfred's shirt was torn from the collar down the front exposing his thin, bony chest covered with long grey hairs.

Wycliffe looked for signs of strangulation but found none.

Alfred had struggled, not with an assailant, but gasping and fighting for air. The experts would say that he had died from suboxia—oxygen deficiency brought about in this case, Wycliffe believed, by a virulent poison. The body was still warm and there were no signs of rigor.

There was a strong smell of brandy and, for the first time, Wycliffe noticed a silvery metal hip-flask lying on the floor, almost under the settee. The stopper was missing and the brandy had trickled out to soak into the sisal matting which covered the floor.

There was nothing he could do but wait, the little hut had been the scene of a violent death and the medical and technical people must have their turn first. All he could do for the moment was to stand in the doorway and look about him.

The hut had been cared for inside as well as out and it was being used. Over the sink at the other end there was a shelf with cups, saucers, and plates; a saucepan hung on a hook and there was a kettle on the oil stove. Close to the door where he stood there was another shelf, this time of books: bird books and others on the identification and habits of small mammals.

Wycliffe went out on the verandah and stood, his arms resting on the rail. Had Alfred committed suicide? That was how it looked. But why come out here to die? Unless there was a strong sentimental attachment to the place. That was possible; after all, the brothers had spent their childhood and youth at Trebyan; perhaps for Alfred the only time of happiness he had known.

But Alfred was a pharmacist; would he have chosen such a terrible death when a narcotic drug would have ensured a tranquil wait for the ferryman and a smooth crossing?

It was quiet, so quiet that Wycliffe listened to the silence and wondered. Occasionally he heard the distant sound of traffic on the main road; now and then a dog barked somewhere in the village. There was a movement in the undergrowth and a rabbit bobbed out into the clearing, settling to feed within a few feet of where he stood.

Had Alfred Glynn murdered his brother then killed himself in this frightful manner by way of expiation? It was as irrational as it was melodramatic, but so was the darkened room where for nearly thirty years Alfred had striven to keep alive the great illusion of his youth.

It occurred to Wycliffe with a sense of surprise that of the three brothers he had spoken only to one; he had never seen either

Matthew or Alfred in life, yet he needed to know them. Physically the brothers had much in common but in personality it seemed they were very different. Matthew was the man of affairs—busy, and apparently untroubled by self-doubt. Alfred had become almost a recluse, a man haunted by his dream. And Maurice . . . ?

Wycliffe looked at his watch and wondered whether Glynn had done what was necessary. The mere fact of Alfred's death, whoever took the call, would be enough for the team to be sent and the police surgeon informed. But that was assuming that the call had been made.

At ten minutes to four he heard a car in the village and a minute or two later it was travelling along the road. Soon it was followed by another. His troops were arriving.

Now the dead man was a centre of attention for the experts. Fox, with his assistants, was searching the whole area and no rabbit would have ventured to show its whiskers.

Lucy Lane was there. "Mr. Kersey is out on enquiries, sir. DC Curnow has stayed at the house to keep an eye on Glynn."

A good job somebody followed proper procedures.

Dr. Rees, the police surgeon, was kneeling beside the body. Rees had spent almost all his professional life in the area and was part of it, ready to applaud its strengths and condone its weaknesses.

"The two brothers inside a couple of days . . . Poor old Alfie! Couldn't take it, I suppose—Matthew on top of everything else. I know there wasn't much love lost between them but, as they say, blood is thicker than water; even doctors know that."

"You said 'on top of everything else'?"

Rees sat back on his haunches. "Well, our lot—the medical practitioners—have been on his tail for years," Rees grinned up at Wycliffe. "A demarcation dispute, you could call it. Alfie was fond of doing our job for us. Then, recently, he went queer—queerer, I should say—and he was stopped from dispensing NHS prescriptions. Quite right, of course, but hard on the old boy."

Rees went on: "Looks as though he laced his brandy. You'd have thought he'd have had more sense."

"More sense?"

"Than to go for strychnine—that's what it looks like to me, and you can see that he had a rough passage out. Conscious to the last probably. Of course with a heart like his it wouldn't have taken long, but why pick on strychnine when he had a fair selection of the British Pharmacopoeia in his dispensary to choose from? But there's no knowing what an intending suicide will do."

"Was he a patient of yours?"

Rees was testing the limbs for flexion. "He wasn't anybody's patient as far as I know. He said he wasn't when he came to see me a couple of years back. Just that one visit. He wanted my opinion of his heart. I examined him and suggested referral to a cardiologist but this he absolutely refused. I told him that in my opinion he was suffering from valvular disease and that there was probably considerable dilation. He said that was what he thought himself. End of story."

"Can you tell me anything about time of death?"

Rees got to his feet. "According to the books strychnine raises the body temperature and so delays cooling. Anyway, rigor is in the very early stages. At a guess I'd say he's probably been dead five or six hours but don't hold me to that. Is Franks going to be in on this?"

"Yes."

"There you are then."

"In the circumstances we have to cover ourselves."

Rees sighed. "Isn't that what we all try to do? . . . You've got a visitor."

Wycliffe turned to look. A young man was standing in the path beyond the clearing just outside the area colonized by the police, tall and slim, dressed in jeans and a denim shirt—no mistaking who he was.

Wycliffe left the hut and walked up to him. "David Glynn?"

The boy nodded.

"Shall we walk a little way?"

A word to Lucy, and Wycliffe walked off up the path with the boy. They stopped just short of where the path ended in the yard.

"Where were you this morning between, say, nine and midday?"

"I was in the house until Chris arrived around ten, then I went to work in the little field behind the house where we grow our vegetables; I was there until nearly one. After a snack lunch I went back there."

"So you were some distance from the hut."

"Quite a way—yes."

The boy had inherited his father's mannerisms as well as his features and physique; a certain hesitancy, and a tendency to look away from the person to whom he was speaking.

"You heard nothing—no cries of distress or anything of that sort?"

"No . . . You think Uncle Alfred suffered a lot?"

"I'm afraid so, but it probably didn't last long and he may not have cried out. Did you have much contact with your uncle?"

"Not much . . . It wasn't very pleasant going there and you tended to put it off . . ."

"And he didn't come here?"

"I've never known him come here until today."

Wycliffe was looking back down the slope, over the gorse towards the trees and beyond, to another clump of trees where the slender grey spire of the church rose above them. "Is this where your Uncle Matthew wanted to build houses?"

"Here and in the adjoining field."

"And your father objected?"

"Yes. Father feels very strongly about this bit of so-called 'waste' ground; so do I."

"Apparently you keep the path clear and look after the little hut; does your father come here much?"

"Never, as far as I know. All the same, for him it's one of those special places." The boy's dark eyes were on Wycliffe, doubtful if he would understand. "I think it's to do with when he was young."

"You spend time at the hut yourself?"

"Yes."

"And not always alone."

The boy turned away.

Wycliffe said: "Let's walk on up to the house. You left Chris at about 10:30 on Saturday night and cycled home?"

"Yes."

"At what time did you get home?"

"About eleven."

"Was your father at home then?"

"Yes."

"Did my brother kill himself?"

"I'm not able to answer that, Mr. Glynn. It seems that he died after drinking brandy which had been laced with strychnine and we have to try to discover how the poison got into the brandy."

"So it's possible that he was murdered?" It was as though the question had been forced from him.

"It is possible but so far there is nothing in the way of evidence to support the idea."

Maurice had been greatly shaken; he was pale and he had difficulty in controlling his voice. He shifted heavily in his chair. "If somebody killed him they must have had a motive, but what? Yet why should he kill himself? And in that horrible way?"

Wycliffe did not answer and after a pause Maurice went on: "What will happen now?"

"We shall treat this as a suspicious death; there will be an autopsy and, of course, an investigation to discover the source of the poison and how it got into the brandy."

They were in what had been the dining-room of the house. An extended dining-table was littered with papers held down by little pottery artefacts from ashtrays to small pitchers and there was a portable typewriter at one end. Dining chairs were scattered about the room; there was a battered filing cabinet with a bulging, open drawer next to a massive sideboard with a marble top. The carpet was threadbare and innocent of pattern, paper was peeling from the walls but there were pictures in gilded frames.

On the mantelpiece, at one end, was the inevitable framed inscribed photograph of Mother; at the other end, a head-and-shoulders portrait of a young woman which caught Wycliffe's attention.

Maurice noticed his interest. "Celia—my wife."

"She was very beautiful."

It was true, but Wycliffe remembered Emily Pascoe's words: ". . . delicate; you could see she wouldn't be long for this world."

The girl in the photograph had a fair fragility, altogether too vulnerable.

"She died when David was four."

Maurice was clearly moved. He fumbled in his jacket pocket and came out with a tobacco pouch and a pipe and offered the pouch to Wycliffe. His hand trembled. "Smoke?"

Wycliffe refused.

"Just as well; I grow my own. Do you mind if I do? It annoys some people—David is one of them."

Maurice concentrated on filling his pipe, very slowly and deliberately; he put the stem between his teeth, and struck a match—a soothing ritual. He was making a tremendous effort to appear calm, if possible to be calm.

He was the last of the brothers; whether or not he had any part in their deaths he could be the key to a clearer understanding of the two who had died. For that reason if for no other it was essential to draw him out rather than subject him to interrogation. Wycliffe sat in an old armchair which had been moulded to comfort through use; his manner relaxed and conversational.

"You had differences with your brother Matthew over possible developments here, I believe?"

"Matthew wanted to build houses. In my view he had no right."

Wycliffe asked no question and, after a pause, Maurice continued: "You see, under my father's will Matthew got the bookshop on condition that he provided for Sara; Alfred had his pharmacy; and this place, where I had already started the pottery, should have been mine. But Father had no faith in my ability to make a go of anything."

A brief pause, perhaps a nervous smile, then: "I've got to admit that there was evidence to support his point of view. I'd made some mistakes and as far as he was concerned the pottery could have been another. Anyway, he left what should have been my share to Matthew on condition that I was able to lease it back at a nominal rental. The point was, he'd made sure I couldn't sell it and blow the proceeds on some other scheme.

"Matthew became my keeper."

Maurice was speaking more slowly; sometimes his lips seemed to tremble but his manner was once more tentative and self-deprecating.

Wycliffe asked: "Did you resent the arrangement?"

Maurice clasped his hands together and seemed to study them. "I don't think so. It gave me a sense of security—security against myself. I couldn't up sticks and away, which I might have done otherwise—regretting it afterwards. But the point was that he was holding this place in trust, on my behalf."

"You thought it unreasonable that he should exploit the property to his advantage—is that it?"

"That was part of it, but I had another and more important reason for opposing him."

"And that was?"

"I think it's time we stopped poisoning half the land and concreting in the rest."

"Where exactly was it proposed these houses should be built?"

"On the scrubland and one of our two fields."

He got up from his chair, fetched a rolled-up plan from the top of the sideboard and spread it over the litter on the table.

"Here." He pointed with his pipe stem.

Wycliffe joined him at the table. The plan showed the outlines of a dozen houses and a service road superimposed on a large-scale map. Wycliffe spotted the little hut and saw that it would be obliterated by one of the proposed houses.

"I gather that your brother may not have made a will; so what happens now?"

"Whether he made a will or not doesn't affect me. Under my father's will, in the event of Matthew's death, the property passes to me anyway." They returned to their seats; Maurice puffed at his pipe and seemed more relaxed.

"If your brother had lived and been granted outline planning permission for his houses, what would you have done?"

Maurice did not hesitate. "I would have gone to law on the terms of my father's will."

Wycliffe changed the subject. "You've lived here alone with your son since your wife died?"

Maurice looked around at the shabby and slightly absurd incongruities of the room. "It's pretty obvious, isn't it? I couldn't afford a housekeeper. In any case if I had any spare money it would go on clerical assistance. Paperwork is our bugbear; we can manage the housekeeping between us. David does a masterly stew and I'm not bad with a salad." His confidence was returning.

"It must have been hard when David was young."

Glynn held his pipe away from his mouth. "I had to take him on more or less from the first. By the time he was two Celia was spending a lot of time in hospitals, poor girl. But people were very good; a friend from the farm came in to help out when I was in a real mess." He smiled a wan smile. "And Sara would take David for days at a time when I was busy in the pottery . . . She's been good to me." He broke off. "There's David now, with Chris."

Wycliffe looked out of the window. The young couple were walking up the drive, arms about each other.

Maurice's eyes were dreamy. "They're like babes in the wood, but they'll be all right. David's got more sense than I ever had and Chris is a good girl. She could make her living as a potter if she wanted to; she's a natural."

"Does she want to?"

"That's what she says but I don't try to influence her either way."

There was a longish pause and this time it was Wycliffe who spoke first. "Do you recall the day your sister-in-law disappeared, Mr. Glynn?"

Maurice seemed startled. "My sister-in-law? Disappearance is hardly the word. She simply left her home and family—"

"That was seventeen years ago and she hasn't as far as I know been seen or heard of since; surely that adds up to a disappearance? Anyway, were you surprised when she went?"

He hesitated. "Of course I was surprised. You don't expect a woman with a young family to simply walk out."

"Can you recollect how your brother reacted?"

"You mean Matthew? Matthew was stunned; he couldn't believe she'd gone. He telephoned me late that evening—when they began to worry about her—asking if she'd been here. She and my wife, Celia, got on fairly well and Inez would sometimes drop in unexpectedly and stay rather long—but never overnight."

"But you hadn't seen her on that occasion?"

"No, I had not."

"And your other brother—Alfred—what about him?"

Maurice shifted heavily in his chair, making the joints creak. "Alfred was bitter; you must know that story by now."

Wycliffe allowed the silence of the place to resume possession. Such silences must have held sway for most of the day in this household of father and son. When Maurice was beginning to get restless Wycliffe said: "Have you ever been over Alfred's rooms above the shop?"

"His rooms? Not all of them. I've been in the living-room—and the kitchen, perhaps. Why?"

"Until very recently the bedroom he intended for Inez and himself was fully furnished, the bed made, pyjamas laid out, fresh flowers and a ticking clock on the bedside table. There were framed photographs of Inez on the walls . . . But it was obvious that the room was never used."

Maurice was watching him, his expression incredulous. He asked in a tight voice: "What do you mean by 'until very recently'?"

"Early this morning or perhaps during the night the room was vandalized; everything in it was either damaged or destroyed."

Maurice's fists were clenched, his features contorted; he got up from his chair and went to the window to stand with his back to the room.

Without turning round he said in a harsh voice: "If you want to know about Inez, Mr. Wycliffe, you must ask Sara, the two of them lived in the same house for nearly twelve years. I don't want to talk about her."

As Wycliffe left the house he looked back and saw the gaunt figure still at the window. He walked down the path to the little hut. Alfred's body had been removed to the mortuary; Fox and Lucy Lane were still there.

Fox said: "We've covered the ground, sir. Deceased's footprints occur in several places along the path between here and the road —wherever the ground is soft enough. I can find no evidence that anyone accompanied him or that anyone met him here."

"Fingerprints?"

"Plenty in the hut but none of them fresh except two or three belonging to the deceased. Other than that, the hip-flask carries the prints of the fingers and thumb of his left hand, and the stopper, of the thumb and forefinger of his right."

"And the other prints in the hut—the old ones?"

"Two people; one male, one female. Well, sir, I've got photographs of the body, of the interior and surroundings of the hut and I'm wondering—"

Wycliffe said: "It's enough to be going on with. Even if we have another homicide on our hands this is not the scene of the crime. Just lock the place and take the key."

CHAPTER SEVEN

Monday afternoon (continued)

Troglodytes in Records had finally unearthed the seventeen-year-old Inez Glynn file. Feet on the table and chair tilted, Kersey settled down to browse. He turned to the last report made by the investigating officer before the file was consigned to Records.

> This investigation, extending over three months, has failed to provide any clue to the present whereabouts of the subject or to suggest any immediate reason why she left her home and family . . .
>
> On the other hand there is no evidence to support the idea of foul play . . . In the past three years subject has been associated with at least two men other than her husband in circumstances giving rise to a strong presumption that the relationships were of a sexual nature . . .
>
> Although she appears to have taken with her no significant quantity of clothing nor any substantial sum of money it seems certain that she was carrying her passport . . .
>
> For reasons set out in earlier reports and in statements (IG 16–19), concerning her car, abandoned in Exeter station carpark, it is possible, even likely that she met someone there by arrangement . . .
>
> Having in mind all the circumstances I suggest that active enquiries in this case be suspended until fresh information is forthcoming.
> (Signed)
> G. M. Marks, Detective Inspector.

Active enquiries were suspended and the file crept farther and farther down the heap until two years after Inez Glynn's disappearance, it had drifted down to archives.

Marks and Kersey had had contact in the distant past. Marks must have retired long since but he might still be around and, on the principle that half an hour's chat over a beer is worth a whole file of police gobbledegook, Kersey decided to enquire and found that Marks was still extant, sharing a bungalow with his sister and her husband in Newlyn. He telephoned.

Marks said: "I'll meet you in the pub in half an hour—The Royal Duke—you know it?"

"No."

"You'll find it."

The Royal Duke was a fishermen's pub with an afternoon trade from men who had brought their catch in during the small hours of the morning. The harbour was crowded with boats berthed two and three abreast but the market sheds were empty, sluiced down so that not even a smell of fish remained. Kersey arrived on time and found Marks already seated at a table by the window with a pint in front of him.

"There's a bitter waiting for you." He signalled the barman; Kersey collected his pint and sat down.

Marks said: "So they made you up to DI."

"Not before time."

Marks had grown greyer, more hairy, more stringy in the years since their last meeting but he was the same man, shrewd, cynical, and a cop to the bone.

"Serious Crimes Squad: you chaps are like Canute these days, trying to hold back the tide."

Kersey, who preferred to do his own job knocking, was curt: "Perhaps, but I haven't got my feet wet yet."

Marks sipped his beer. "So you want to hear about Inez."

"What sort of woman was she?"

"The sort some men will sit up and beg for while others run; it wasn't only looks, she had style." Marks broke off to acknowledge a greeting from a newcomer who went to the bar. "Why she picked on the Glynns, God only knows. She was thirty-six when she cleared out and she'd had three kids, but she still made younger women look and feel like there was no contest."

"You say she cleared out; I suppose you looked at the possibility that she went—wherever she did go—not of her own free will?"

Marks showed his spines. "Look here, boy, I wasn't wet behind the ears then and I'm not now! Anyway you can have it as I got it. Inez was friendly with a woman living in Hayle and she used to visit pretty often, usually on Sundays; occasionally she would stay overnight. Anyway, that's what she told her husband.

"Matthew knew it was sometimes genuine, sometimes an alibi." Marks made a dismissive gesture. "Didn't bother him; he'd reached that point. As long as she kept the action out of town."

Marks took a gulp of beer and wiped his moustache. "Anyway this Sunday evening she didn't turn up and the woman in Hayle hadn't seen her—hadn't expected her. The last the family ever saw of Inez was when she set off in her little red Mini Sunday morning with twenty quid in her purse and her passport."

"Was that the last report of anybody seeing her?"

"Almost. A woman friend saw her driving out of town a few minutes later; after that she just vanished into thin air. Your shout, I think."

Kersey went to the bar and had to wait while a group of fishermen jointly related to the landlord a story of putting into an Irish port for shelter and being suspected by the Garda of gunrunning for the IRA.

He was attended to at last and returned to his table with the drinks. The pub was filling and the smoke haze thickened as spirits rose.

Marks said: "Good prices for this morning's landings." He sipped his beer and resumed where he had left off. "Matthew notified us Monday morning and her car was reported in Exeter station car-park on Thursday—been there since Monday morning at least. The attendant reported it when news of our interest in red Minis filtered through."

Kersey said: "So somebody drove the Mini to Exeter—could it have been anybody other than Inez?"

Marks was po-faced. "Could've been, but nothing to suggest that it was: her prints were all over the car and nobody else's."

Kersey said: "Easy enough to fix for anybody with reason to."

"I'm not denying it, but you've got to see it from our point of view at the time. Nobody seemed all that surprised at her pushing off."

"Did she have any relatives? I mean, did you come across any?"

"Her mother—a widow and remarried, living somewhere in Kent—and a sister, married, with four children, in Nottingham. Neither of them wanted to know about Inez."

Marks was watching a young fisherman in the act of draining a pint tankard without swallowing. "I could do that once . . . No there was nobody overcome with anxiety it seemed to me, not even her husband."

"Leaving aside what you thought at the time, and looking back, could he have driven the car to Exeter after disposing of his wife?"

Marks took his time. "That raises a question. She left home that Sunday morning all right—no doubt about that. How would he pick her up again? By appointment?"

"He could have known where she was going."

"Even if he did it seems a bit far-fetched to think he could do anything about it. But, allowing that he could, he might just about have been able to drive the car to Exeter Sunday night. It's a hundred and twenty miles—say up to three hours in that little crate—and he could make the night train down, arriving home in the early morning and, with luck, not being recognized by anybody on the trip or at the station, and not disturbing the family."

Meditative, Marks drew his finger around the rim of his glass. "It's not on, boy!"

"Is that all you've got to tell me?"

"There was one thing that struck me as a bit odd when I had a chance to look back on it. I had a phone call from a chap called Armitage—Colonel Armitage—asking about her. He was the son of the old lady Inez was companion to before she married Glynn. The colonel said Inez was a distant relative and he wanted to know if there was anything odd about her disappearance. I couldn't quite make out what he was after. Anyway I gave him the gist of what had happened and he asked me if I would let him know if we found her."

"Where did this colonel live?"

"Somewhere in London then; it's probably in the files but it's unlikely he's there now. I've got an idea they're a Cornish family and that's why the old lady was here in the first place."

Kersey said: "So on the basis of what you've told me you concluded that Inez was off to join her boyfriend in Exeter—is that it?"

"No, it bloody well isn't, not altogether. All this happened in early spring—the third week in March, I think—and for several weeks of the previous summer Inez had been carrying on with a man staying at one of the St. Ives hotels. In the course of our investigation it turned out that this character had been lying low, wanted by Bristol CID on fraud charges." Marks drained his glass. "He wasn't seen again either. Are you having another?"

"No thanks. I've had my ration."

Marks looked at him with a speculative eye. "Let's see, you got married or something didn't you?"

"I got married."

"Still with it?"

"Yes."

"Any kids?"

"Two girls at university."

Marks nodded. "Wish I had. I'm living with my sister; she's got a boy and a girl but it's not the same."

"About this guy in the St. Ives hotel—was there any evidence to suggest that he and Inez kept in touch?"

"Not directly but we did find out that Inez had been getting letters with Spanish stamps."

"And Spain was a cosy hideaway for our export villains; *ergo*, her boyfriend was waiting for her to join him on the Costa del Crook."

Marks was nettled. "You can laugh, boy, but this was seventeen years ago. We weren't still in the push-bike and whistle era down here but neither did we have whiz kids from the crime squad on our doorstep to tell us what to do and how to do it. It was a different ball-game in those days and you bloody well know it."

When Wycliffe returned to the Incident Room the printer, like all the other business people in the town, had closed his shop and gone home, but two reporters were keeping vigil.

"Suicide, Mr. Wycliffe?"

"I don't know."

"He was poisoned?"

"Yes, the signs are that he died as a result of poisoning but this has to be confirmed."

"Will your investigation into the murder of Matthew Glynn continue or do you regard the case as closed?"

"The investigation will certainly continue."

"Is it true that there was a long-standing feud between the two brothers?"

"The word 'feud' suggests a degree of acrimony for which I've found no evidence."

Policemen are becoming as adept at verbal evasion as politicians, far outstripping bishops and trade union leaders.

Potter, the squad's fat man, was duty officer. "There are several memos and reports on your desk, sir."

"Is there any coffee going?"

"I'll bring it up, sir."

Wycliffe skimmed through the accumulated paper on his table, pushed it aside, got up, and walked to the window where he stood, looking out.

The sun was low in the sky somewhere away to his right, and the castle on the Mount was bathed in magical golden light. On the south coast of the county, when the weather is sunny and calm, the hour before dusk induces a mood of solemnity. In the offices of the church it is the turn of Vespers. Wycliffe was always reminded of the hymn which sang of "saints casting down their golden crowns around the glassy sea." The image depressed him; if that was heaven it was best left to the cherubim and seraphim who might be turned on by that sort of thing.

Potter came in and concluded that his chief was absorbed in profound cerebration; he put the coffee on the table and crept out . . .

Kersey arrived. "I gather I missed the excitement."

Wycliffe turned away from the window with a sigh.

Kersey asked: "Are we still looking for the killer of Matthew Glynn?"

"You're no better than the reporters! I'd like to be a hundred percent sure that Alfred killed himself."

"There's a doubt?"

"There's bound to be. Would you choose strychnine as a way out? And would you go for a bus ride followed by a longish walk to take the fatal dose in a little hut in the middle of nowhere?"

"From what we hear Alfred wasn't exactly rational."

"Perhaps not, and he may have had sentimental reasons for going to the little hut, but I want to be sure. Anyway, I gather you've been delving into prehistory—Marks, wasn't it? I remember him vaguely. What did you make of it?"

Kersey lit a cigarette. "I don't think they had enough hard evidence to conclude that Inez ran off with or to another man. Or, in fact, that she ran off at all."

"Her car?"

"Anybody could have driven it to Exeter and dumped it at the station without leaving traces that would be discovered by anything short of a pukka forensic examination."

"Are you suggesting that she was murdered and that the car business was a cover-up?"

"I'm saying that there was no real evidence against that as a possibility. I'm not carping about the way Marks handled the case; an adult woman went missing in circumstances which seemed to offer a plausible explanation. To me, the fact that she hasn't been heard of again in seventeen years puts a different complexion on it. She would be fifty-three or -four now and I find it difficult to believe that any woman who has had three children wouldn't show some curiosity about what happened to them once the glamour of life had worn a bit thin."

Wycliffe was silent for a while, engaged in such crucial activities as straightening his telephone flex, boxing up the heap of papers on his desk into a tidy pile, and scratching his chin. Kersey blew smoke rings and watched them with approval.

Finally Wycliffe said: "There must be people still living in this town who knew her well. It should be possible to find out more about the woman from sources less prejudiced than the family."

"The whole thing could turn out to be a mare's nest."

"Very likely, but anything you do find out could throw light on the family. See what you can do in a couple of days."

"A free hand?"

"A free hand. Anything else?"

"Just another thing which could be something or nothing. While Marks's inquiry into Inez's disappearance was going on he had a call from a Colonel Armitage, son of the old lady Inez lived with before she married."

"Saying what?"

"Nothing much, really just asking to be told if they found her."

"It could be worth contacting this colonel. If he's still around it shouldn't be difficult. As a last resort MOD might tell us if we filled in the right forms. See what you can do. If you locate him we'll send someone to interview him."

Kersey left, and was back in less than ten minutes. "I found our colonel in the phone book; I remembered old Marks saying he thought they might be a Cornish family. Anyway he's living at Helford, near Falmouth: Colonel Anthony Armitage, CBE, DSO, Ponsyn Cottage."

"He might not be our man."

"He is; I phoned. A woman answered and she agreed that his mother had lived in Penzance. He's out at the moment but he'll be in later and he'll phone either tonight or in the morning."

Wycliffe passed an uneasy night. Names and faces, phrases and vivid little pictures presented themselves to his mind in a constant succession of changing patterns like the images in a kaleidoscope. Sara, the worthy virgin, self-absorbed but acute: ". . . my sister-in-law was a very remarkable woman." Gerald, pretending to a *savoir faire* he did not possess: "I suppose somebody could have been in there doing the old man while I was trying to get in . . ." Young David Glynn: ". . . for Dad it is one of those special places." The scared look on the girl's face when she caught sight of Wycliffe in the yard. Maurice Glynn: "Matthew was my keeper." The manuscript books with their red bindings which he had not actually seen. Sara again: "No, there was no crisis . . ." The darkened room with the double bed and the fresh, red carnations at the bedside, viciously destroyed. Swayne: "Well, there was a wedding all right but it was Matthew who married the girl." Alfred's contorted body lying in the little hut. Barry Morse quoted by Kersey: "It lends new meaning to the phrase 'keeping a shop.' " And Lucy Lane: "I wonder he didn't cash in on the journals."

Did all the pieces belong to one puzzle? Only experience saved him from despairing at this rag-bag of memories.

At a quarter to four by the little travelling clock at his bedside he got out of bed and went to the window. He had sensed a change in the air, a salty dampness. At the open casement a gentle breeze blew a mist of fine rain into his face. Although there was no moon to be seen it was far from totally dark; the sea was dimly luminescent while shapes and shadows defined the land. An intermittent glow in the south-east marked the sweep of the Lizard Light while nearer to hand the harbour lights and the streetlamps contributed patches of misty radiance. He closed the casement and went back to bed and to sleep.

Next morning the whole town and bay were shrouded in mist which condensed on every cold surface. The Mount was a shadow in the air and the iron railings along the promenade dripped globules of moisture. Wycliffe walked to work with a salty taste on his lips and arrived at the Incident Room as the little printer was opening up.

At a quarter to nine he was joined in his office by Kersey. "Good morning, sir." Very formal and polite. Kersey liked to discharge his obligations to the hierarchy early in the day; after that he felt free to speak his mind man to man.

He pulled up a chair and sat down. "I was going through the reports, trying to size up Matthew Glynn—what made him tick. On the face of it his life centred around business of one sort or another, his own and the council's. He had plenty of acquaintances but just a couple of friends—Swayne, the stamp man, and Doble, the wine merchant. Apart from the weekly chess session he seems to have had no hobby, no what you might call recreation." Kersey's rubbery features creased in a ferocious grin. "I mean, a double bed made up for one. After all he was only fifty-two and I'm forty-eight."

Wycliffe said: "He took two holidays a year: a spring fortnight abroad and an autumn fortnight in this country."

"Alone?"

"Apparently."

"Well, it helps to fill in the picture but I haven't finished yet. He had a car—a Volvo 244, five years old with only twelve thousand miles on the clock. According to the family he rarely used it except on Sundays when he spent the afternoon and evening with an old chap who used to work for the firm and now lives in sheltered accommodation at Carbis Bay. He would leave home immediately after lunch and come back between ten and eleven at night."

Wycliffe was unresponsive; his look said: "Are we getting there?"

"The point is, I rang the accommodation warden just to check; Matthew did visit the old boy every Sunday but he never spent more than half an hour with him. He would hand over the old man's baccy for the week and a few sweeties then, after a bit of chat, he was away."

Kersey looked at Wycliffe, expecting some question or comment and when none came he went on: "So where did he spend his time after lunch each Sunday?"

"I don't know but you're going to tell me."

"I'm not, but I'm sending Curnow to Carbis Bay to talk to the old man. It's possible he might know something."

Wycliffe remembered the seemingly expensive package tour to Bulgaria, booked with—was it Eurotravel? He reached for the telephone. "Get me the Penzance office of Eurotravel please." He replaced the phone and explained to Kersey. "This may save Curnow a trip."

The phone rang: Eurotravel had no local office; the nearest was Truro. That in itself might mean something. "Get me the manager of the Truro office."

A minute or two later he was speaking to a suave gentleman anxious to steer a safe course between Scylla and Charybdis. "We do have to observe client confidentiality . . ."

"But your client is dead—murdered."

"Yes, but a second person may be involved—"

"And that person could be a key witness in our investigation; but if you insist on a Court Order . . ."

"No! no, of course we wouldn't want to do that. If you will hold for a moment . . ."

It came at last: "Mr. Glynn's travelling companion was to be a Mrs. Florence Tremayne of Nansallas Cottage, New Mill."

"Was Mr. Glynn a regular customer of yours?"

"Every year as regular as clockwork—ever since I've been here, and that's eight years."

"With the same companion?"

"Always."

Wycliffe replaced the phone. "There we are then."

"They must have been very discreet. Are you going to telephone her?"

"No, I'll pay a call this afternoon."

Kersey left and the telephone rang again. "Wycliffe."

It was Franks, the pathologist. "Well, Charles, I've taken a good look at your latest victim. Of course I've sent specimens to Forensic but you can take it from me that he died of strychnine poisoning; a fairly hefty dose but he'd been living on borrowed time anyway. The Old Reaper would have caught up with him in weeks, probably, months at most. Talk about dilation!"

There were times when he felt cut off by some imponderable barrier; the usual sights and sounds reached him but they seemed to do so through a screen of interference, like a badly tuned radio. He could sympathize with the computer that puts up its little sign, "Memory full."

It was ten o'clock; he went into the outer room and muttered to the duty officer: "I shall be at the pharmacy."

Fox was already there with a pharmacologist from the county hospital who was looking at Alfred's stock of drugs with a view to discovering a possible source of the poison.

Wycliffe left the Incident Room and walked up the steep alley to Lady Street, into the usual morning clutter of delivery vans and pedestrians. Alfred's shop looked as though it had been closed and deserted for months; it was hard to believe that it was only three days since a few people, at least, had been entering through the rickety door with its small glass panes to buy patent medicines or seek advice. Somebody had put a notice inside the glass, "Closed indefinitely."

Wycliffe went round the back, rang the doorbell, and was admitted by one of Fox's assistants. "The sergeant is in the shop, sir. Shall I fetch him?"

"No."

He climbed the stairs, went through the living-room where nothing seemed to have changed, and down to the shop. Fox met him at the bottom of the stairs. Through the glass partition they could see the pharmacologist busy in the dispensary.

Fox said: "He was like a hungry dog let loose in a butcher's shop; not knowing where to start. He says he's never seen anything like it; he reckons some of the stuff must have been here since before the First World War. 'A profile of pharmaceutical dispensing over eighty years'—that's what he called it. Odd, the things people get worked up about."

"I'll have a word. What's his name?"

"Edmunds, sir—Dr. Edmunds."

Edmunds was thirtyish, bearded, slim, and earnest; one of the modern breed of technical scientists who believe that the ultimate secret of life, the universe and all that, must be reducible to the predictable antics of their molecules and atoms and the infuriatingly ambiguous particles which seem to compose them.

He waited for no introduction but launched into his current theme: "It's amazing! Most of this stuff must have been here long before Glynn took over the business; it's a museum of pharmaceutical archaeology—"

"About the strychnine—"

"Yes, of course. Well, at one time—into the sixties, actually—strychnine was used as a heart stimulant and in so-called 'tonic' medicines. In fact, it has no medical value whatever and it is an extremely dangerous drug to have lying around. It is one of the alkaloids derived from certain plant tissues but synthesized in the fifties—"

"And there is strychnine amongst this lot?"

"Oh, yes: two sources actually; a dry extract of nux vomica— that is to say of the ground-up seeds of the plant; this contains about five percent strychnine; and a preparation known as liquor strychnine hydrochloride which contains about one percent of the hydrochloride."

Fox spoke up. "I examined the two bottles for prints and found nothing identifiable on the hydrochloride, but on the nux vomica bottle there were fresh prints of the deceased's left hand and on the stopper good prints of the forefinger and thumb of his right hand. Also the stopper came out easily while most of the others were stuck."

Edmunds went on in his lecture-room style as though Fox had not interrupted: "Either form of the poison could have been administered in brandy but brandy would not by any means completely mask the bitter taste." He added, generously: "You may know that it was the bitter taste which made it unpopular with poisoners of the past even when it was fairly freely available."

So Alfred had laced his own brandy and taken it to the little hut which had youthful associations, there to kill himself in a manner that was almost ceremonial. Did it really matter from which bottle the stuff had come? But the courts like to know these things; it creates a comfortable illusion of precision and that's what justice is about. You can't put emotions in a bottle labelled "Exhibit B."

As Wycliffe was about to leave, the telephone rang in the little office next to the dispensary. Fox answered it and signalled through the glass partition.

"DS Lane, sir."

Lucy sounded mildly excited. "Sara is here, sir. She says she wants to make a statement."

"So what's to stop her?"

"She will only make it to you."

"What's she like—uptight?"

"That about describes it, not exactly agitated, but disturbed."

"All right; I'll be there shortly. Put her in my office with a WPC if you can find one." He turned back to Fox. "When you've finished here you've got Matthew Glynn's attic where all Inez's stuff is stored."

Wycliffe got Fox to let him out by the shop door. Despite the misty rain the street was busy; the pubs had chalk-boards outside advertising their lunchtime menus; two of the shops had scaffolding against them, getting a face-lift before the start of the season. He turned down the alley which led to the Incident Room. The printer had become sufficiently reconciled to their presence to give him a friendly wave.

Lucy Lane was waiting for him.

"I want you in on this. I'll talk to her; I'd rather you didn't butt in at this stage—and nothing for the record. Afterwards you can take her statement."

Sara was sitting on one of the bentwood chairs by the desk in the bare little office; a WPC, her black-stockinged legs tucked under her chair, sat by the door. She stood up as Wycliffe came in followed by Lucy Lane.

"You can go. Tell them I don't want to be disturbed."

Sara wore a thin mackintosh over a blouse and skirt; her handbag was on the floor at her side and a furled umbrella rested against the desk. She looked very pale and drawn, almost haggard.

Lucy Lane took the seat by the door; Wycliffe settled behind his desk. "You wished to see me, Miss Glynn?"

His manner was formal.

"You suggested that I should make a fresh statement."

"Perhaps you will tell me what it is you have to say?"

Sara was holding a pair of suede gloves crushed in one hand. "What I told you about Saturday night—going out to post letters and afterwards going for a walk—was perfectly true." She looked across the desk at Wycliffe as though for encouragement, but none came; his expression remained bland; she could not even be sure that he was looking at her or whether his gaze was focused on the window behind her.

"But I did not tell you—" She broke off, distressed. "I did not tell you that, on the way back, as I came round the church into the lane, I saw Alfred coming out of our back door . . . He came down the lane towards me like a man sleep-walking. I spoke to him but he walked past me as though I wasn't there . . . I watched him go in by his own back door and I hurried on home. I couldn't imagine what had happened . . . I mean, I don't think Alfred had been in the house or the bookshop except for Mother's Wednesday teas since we moved from Trebyan nearly thirty years ago."

Sara stopped speaking and the silence was broken only by the thudding of the printing press below. She was kneading the gloves in her lap, gripping them so tightly that her knuckles showed white. Lucy Lane, on the point of speaking, changed her mind. Wycliffe gave no sign, and Sara was left with no option but to continue.

"I was afraid something had happened but I never imagined anything so . . . so awful. I saw the light in Matthew's office and I went—"

"Did you bolt the yard door behind you?"

"Yes, I did."

"Why?"

She looked vague, troubled. "I don't know; I was frightened, it seemed the thing to do . . ."

"Go on."

She looked down at her lap. "I went to the door of Matthew's office and opened it . . ."

"Did you go in?"

"There was no need. I could see him . . ."

"Did you see the cat?"

"The cat? Yes, it slipped past me as I opened the door."

"All right; go on."

"Well, I shut the door, crossed the yard, and let myself in through the kitchen. There was no one about . . . I went upstairs to my room." She took a handkerchief from her sleeve and put it to her eyes, shaking her head. "I couldn't face any more . . . I couldn't! . . . And I had to decide what I should say . . . It was a terrible night!"

"And in the morning?"

She raised her eyes. "As soon as it was light I went downstairs . . . I pretended to find Matthew and I roused the family . . ."

It was as though Wycliffe was giving her only part of his attention; he seemed to have become absorbed in his own thoughts and when Sara stopped speaking there was an interval long enough for Lucy Lane to look at him with concern. When he spoke it was abruptly and with a complete change of subject: "It seems that the little hut at Trebyan meant a lot to your brothers."

"The hut?" Sara was surprised, startled by the abrupt change. She said: "Yes, I suppose it did, when they were young."

"Did you spend much time there?"

"No, it was the boys' place. They used to camp out there in the summer holidays."

Wycliffe could not imagine Sara camping out anywhere or at any stage of her life.

"And as they got older? They must have been in their twenties when the family moved from Trebyan."

Sara carefully separated her gloves which she had rolled up into a ball. Without looking up she said: "I don't know what you are getting at, Mr. Wycliffe; all this was a long time ago."

"Did they meet their girlfriends in the hut?"

"I've no idea." Very prim.

"Did they bring their friends home—to the house?"

"No; my father was not—" She broke off.

"You were going to say?"

"Nothing. I can see no point in these questions. I have told you what happened on Saturday night and I am willing to answer questions about it."

Wycliffe looked at her, his grey eyes brooding and expressionless. Sara puzzled him; he had underestimated her. He said: "When your brother Maurice's wife was ill and David was an infant I understand you looked after him from time to time."

"I did what I could."

"Just one more question, Miss Glynn: when your brother Alfred visited his mother while Inez was still with you, did they have any contact?"

A vigorous shake of the head. "No. Alfred would never acknowledge that she existed."

Alone, he went to stand by the window, looking out. Standing at windows was his favourite situation for brooding, self-examination, consoling or condemning himself . . . wondering what to do next.

It was still misty but the sun was gathering strength and the mist had acquired a pearly hue promising better things.

Sara's story made sense; it made sense in the context of Alfred's bizarre existence. Matthew Glynn had been strangled by his brother Alfred because . . . Alfred Glynn had killed himself because . . . And Sara's story explained her own ambivalent behaviour . . . Tidy. Convincing. He had no doubt that the case could be wound up on the strength of it. No trial; you can't try a dead man. The facts were accounted for and Sara's evidence at the inquest would clinch it . . .

But there were other facts: Inez Glynn had disappeared; but that was seventeen years ago. Maurice Glynn had quarrelled with his brother: obviously a coincidence. There was the unexplained presence of a nineteenth-century journal in Matthew's safe: nothing to do with the case. And there was the little hut . . . He didn't know himself what he meant by that . . . Wycliffian dialectic.

He sighed. All the same he was going to take another look.

CHAPTER EIGHT

Tuesday morning

The telephone rang and he went back to his desk. A wary duty officer said: "A Colonel Armitage is here asking to see you, sir."

Wycliffe went through to the little room which had been set aside for callers. "Colonel Armitage? . . . Wycliffe. Good of you to come."

Armitage was by no means the popular image of a colonel, irascible and autocratic; he was thin, elderly, and mild-mannered; he looked more like an old-style academic who had acquired his pale-parchment skin through years of desiccation in college libraries; but his eyes were full of vitality.

"My housekeeper drove me in—I'm not safe on the roads any more." With his long, scrawny neck and high-pitched voice, he suggested to Wycliffe an aristocratic parrot. "Now I spend all the time I can on the water—more room." A friendly grin exposing yellowed but home-grown teeth.

Wycliffe led him into his office and entered upon the preamble: "In a murder case we have to follow every possible lead. We are in touch with you because your name cropped up in reports concerning the disappearance of the murdered man's wife. That, of course, was seventeen years ago. I understand that Inez Glynn, prior to her marriage, was your mother's housekeeper-companion."

The colonel nodded. "Quite so. Inez was with Mother until she died. It was shortly afterwards that she married the bookseller."

"And twelve years on, when Inez disappeared, you still expressed an interest."

"Yes, I did." Armitage marshalled his ideas. "In the first place,

Inez was a distant relative—some sort of cousin—but I must confess to another more direct motive. When my mother died I was a military attaché at one of our embassies in eastern Europe. It was at the time of the Bulganin-Khruschev circus and my leave was very short—not long enough to clear up my mother's affairs as I wished to do.

"Subsequently I was disappointed to find that some of our family papers were missing. I approached Inez, then Mrs. Matthew Glynn, and she told me that she knew nothing of them. Of course I was not in a position to contradict her."

"But you did not believe in her ignorance."

Armitage spread his thin hands. "That is putting it rather more strongly than I would have done. Years later, when I heard that Inez had left her husband and that the police were investigating her disappearance, I was tempted to carry the matter a little further. However, it soon became obvious that Inez was not to be found, and everything I learned about Matthew Glynn convinced me that he was an honest man." The colonel shrugged. "In the circumstances there was no more to be done and I put the matter out of my mind until your officer telephoned my housekeeper yesterday."

Wycliffe said: "Will you tell me the nature of the missing papers?"

Armitage seemed almost as interested in the coloured stencilled designs which decorated the peeling walls as in the subject being discussed. He recovered his manners in polite confusion. "Of course! They concerned my mother's paternal grandfather, who had spent a great many years in southern Africa—Natal and Cape Colony. They comprised his journal—a fairly detailed and animated account of his life during nearly forty years up to about 1890—and his letter books, with copies of his correspondence. In his later years, he was closely associated with Cecil Rhodes so these records might have some historical as well as family interest."

"And considerable monetary value?"

"I suppose so—yes."

"Was your great grandfather Martin J. Beale?"

Armitage looked at him in astonishment. "Yes, indeed."

"Then his journal is in Glynn's safe under seal at the moment."

"You amaze me! I had no idea that my coming here would lead to anything of the sort."

"The letter books you mention are not there."

"No matter! I'm delighted to recover . . . I suppose I shall be able to recover the journal?"

"I've no doubt of that but you will have to deal with the family or with their solicitor. Was there anything else that you expected to find amongst your mother's papers that you did not?"

The colonel frowned. "Yes, there was a collection of letters written by Martin Beale to his mother; they were of purely family interest, kept by her out of sentiment I suppose. After all, South Africa was a long way off in those days and home leave must have been a great rarity."

They parted company, pleased with themselves and with each other.

It was past two when Wycliffe and Kersey made it to a pub for lunch; a pub not far from the bookshop. They had a table by the window in an upstairs room decorated with a random collection of memorabilia from a colourful maritime past. Outside the window, on a flat roof, seagulls strutted up and down eyeing inaccessible snacks like Dickensian children pressing their noses against pastry-shop windows.

Wycliffe brought Kersey up to date but seemed reluctant to enter into any sort of discussion. Kersey watched the gulls and tried various gambits to draw him out, succeeding at last: "I suppose Sara's story is credible and you can't altogether blame her for not coming out with it sooner."

"No."

"Unless she killed Matthew and Alfred's death gave her a heaven-sent scapegoat."

Wycliffe made a gesture of rejection. "I don't think Sara was Matthew's killer. Look at the facts: she was seen in Alexandra Road at 11:15, the very time at which Gerald found the yard door barred against him. Fifteen minutes later, a woman, who could only have been Sara, found the door unbarred. It seems to me highly likely that the killer had locked himself in and that he got away during that fifteen minutes."

"And that Sara met him?"

"That's another matter but it's quite possible."

"So where does that leave us? What's the next move?"

"My next move is to talk to Matthew's woman friend—Florence Tremayne—isn't that her name? Your job is to get what you can on Inez."

Kersey sprinkled sugar on his apple pie. "Yes, I've got a lead there. There's an old lady living next door to what used to be the Armitage house; she was there when Mrs. Armitage was alive and Inez was her companion."

"Could she tell you anything?"

"Not much, but it seems that her daughter and Inez were close, and remained friendly after both of them married. I gather the old lady didn't approve. Anyway, the daughter now has grown-up children and is living in Launceston. I thought of going over there this afternoon."

"Good! There's one other thing: can you recall Maurice's account of how he spent Saturday evening?"

"I can check the report but I think he was in the pub at Gold-sithney until nineish then he went home."

"Driving the Land Rover?"

"No, he had a push-bike. Why?"

"I wondered."

A little later Kersey tried again: "At least we know how Matthew got hold of the Beale journal and why he kept it under wraps. From what Morse said it looks as though he was trying to flog it in some under-the-counter deal, but I don't see how it helps us."

"No."

"You're not having any dessert? This pie is good."

"Only coffee."

"New Mill—do you know where it is?"

Lucy Lane was driving Wycliffe's car. "I've got a cousin who farms not far from the village and I used to stay there in the holidays when I was a girl."

Lucy's relatives seemed to be uniformly and conveniently distributed throughout the south-western peninsula.

"But you don't happen to know the lady we are going to see?"

"I'm afraid not, sir."

Lucy Lane had been working in his team for three years but he felt that he knew her only a little better than he had done after her first month. She was a workaholic, highly intelligent, and singularly free from hang-ups, but there was a barrier. Sometimes he thought it was of his own making: he was unaccustomed to working closely with women and this one was still young and attractive which made him self-conscious.

The road was narrow, no more than a lane, prone to cows and farm tractors, but Lucy drove with a relaxed confidence which he envied. He had never achieved a rapport with the automobile and avoided the driving seat when he could.

New Mill consists of a straggle of houses following the course of the lane and a stream. Like much of Penwith it has a powerful ethos which refuses to be submerged by the modern world; the countryside is littered with artefacts spanning the centuries, from megalithic chamber tombs to nineteenth-century mine workings, and only the moron can escape a sense of continuity with and obligation to the past. If Glynn had wanted a cover for visits to his woman friend, his charitable trips to St. Ives served him well; New Mill involved only a detour of a mile or so from the direct route.

"It's some distance beyond the village, by the stream." Lucy had this from a man weeding his garden.

In fact the stream ran through Florence Tremayne's garden which was a wild garden with trees and an abundance of daffodils. The cottage itself was severe, a slate-roofed little building in the Cornish tradition, but its walls were covered with creepers now coming into leaf.

A neatly written notice on the door read: "Knock and if there's no answer come round the back."

There was an answer.

"Mrs. Tremayne? . . . Chief Superintendent Wycliffe; this is Detective Sergeant Lane . . ."

She did not look like a predatory widow and she was no super-annuated dolly-bird either; she must have been fifty, she was on the plump side, clear skinned, with a frank, open face. She wore trousers and a smock.

"I was expecting somebody, I suppose. You'd better come in."

They were shown into a room which ran the whole depth of the cottage, bright and chintzy, the indoor equivalent of a herbaceous border. There were daffodils in vases and framed flower-paintings on the walls.

"You didn't think to get in touch with us, Mrs. Tremayne?"

She was sitting on a gaily upholstered settee while Wycliffe and Lucy Lane had the two matching armchairs. "Yes, I thought about it but I decided that the family had enough to put up with without learning about me. It isn't as though I could tell you anything that would help to explain what happened to Matt."

Her manner was restrained; sad but not grief-stricken. Wycliffe felt sure that in normal circumstances she was a cheerful woman, more ready to laugh than cry. "I should explain that Matt and I were not lovers in the accepted sense; we were friends—good friends, we'd known each other from childhood so we had a lot in common. I was born and brought up in St. Hilary Parish; my maiden name was Scoble and Father farmed Little Carn. Most of the older people in the parish remember me as Florrie Scoble."

The sun was shining through the little window making patterns of light and shadow on the carpet and causing the polished wood-work to glow.

"You've been in contact with Matthew Glynn all through?"

"Oh, no! When Matt married Inez I was left high and dry. A year later I met a sales rep for an agricultural firm and married him. You could say it was on the rebound but I had no reason to regret it. We moved to Somerset and I saw nothing of Matt for—I don't know—it must've been sixteen years I suppose. My husband was killed in a road accident in '71 and I couldn't bear to live on alone up there so I bought this place—returning to the scenes of my youth, or very nearly."

She had a mop of unruly brown hair, streaked with grey, and she swept it back from her face with an impatient movement that was wholly girlish.

Wycliffe said: "You implied that you and Matthew were plan-ning to marry when he married Inez—is that so?"

"Oh, yes; at least that was my impression." A helpless gesture. "And Inez was supposed to be marrying Alfred."

"Was it a complete surprise to you when Matthew and Inez agreed to marry?"

For the first time she hesitated. "Oh, dear! This is really probing the old wound. I had no idea it could still hurt. I knew that Inez had had her turn in the little hut but I didn't know until afterwards that she was pregnant. Yes, when Matt told me he was going to marry her it was a surprise—a shock." She looked at him, questioning. "I suppose you know about the little hut?"

"It's still there."

She looked down at her hands. "I know. It sounds quite absurd but the other day I walked up the footpath from the road just to see if it was. A boy came out and looked at me, a bit suspicious, and I felt a fool, but that boy took me back thirty years. He could have been any one of the brothers. Of course, it was Maurice's boy.

"Anyway, the hut looked just the same; things wear better than people, don't they?"

"You have memories of the little hut?"

She coloured and laughed. "When I remember it first it was a playroom for the Glynn children and any others they cared to let in; a sort of clubhouse. Later, as the boys became teenagers and young men, it became a place for them to meet their girlfriends.

"Perhaps it's difficult to believe now, but the Glynn boys could take their pick of girls. Of course Matt was regarded as the prize and I suppose I was flattered when he became serious with me—or seemed to."

Wycliffe said: "And you met Matthew again when you came back here to live?"

"Within a year or so; a chance meeting."

"And that started the Sunday visits and the biannual holidays?"

A short laugh. "So you know our secrets. I suppose you must, since you're here. Anyway, that was all he wanted of me though he offered marriage. He didn't really want a deeper involvement."

"And you?"

"Oh, I would have turned him down anyway. Meeting Matthew again after sixteen years of marriage and hearing about the rest of the family—it made me realize there was something about the Glynns . . ."

"What kind of thing?"

She was picking at a loose cotton in the hem of her smock. "I can't quite explain it. When I think back it seems to me they were all three of them looking for a groove to settle in—tramlines that would take them somewhere without them having to think where they were going." She laughed at her own image. "They might have to work—the Glynns aren't lazy—but they want to make their decisions once and for all." She looked up, questioning, wondering if she had made sense.

Wycliffe watched her, dreamy-eyed; it was impossible to say whether he was interested or not, even whether he was really listening. Lucy Lane wondered, not for the first time, what it was about him that encouraged people to talk; sometimes it was almost as though he wasn't there.

Florrie Tremayne went on regardless: "And poor old Alfred with his shop; he'd wanted to be a doctor, a GP, plodding along in some backwater for forty years, supported by a sufficient number of loyal patients who hung on his words and swallowed his medicines with no fuss. Instead, he had to settle for a chemist's shop, and though he still tried to behave like a doctor, it didn't work. To make a living he had to sell things over the counter—like his brother."

Lucy Lane said: "But apart from that there was a sort of tragedy in his life—at least he saw it as one."

Florrie looked at the girl. "You really think so? You may be right but some people seem to dramatize a commonplace misfortune and turn it into a cult. They live on it. I may be hard, but it looks to me like an excuse for not facing the real world—perhaps a welcome excuse."

"What about Maurice? Has he found his groove?" It was Wycliffe, giving the first indication that he had followed her argument, and she became flustered. It was almost as though he was consulting her.

She said: "Oh, I think so—he was upset enough at the idea of Matt building houses next to his pottery, wasn't he?"

"Upset enough to kill?" The question came quietly, almost casually, but if Florrie had been flustered before, now she was shocked. "The idea had never entered my head! I know it's not your fault, but you come here and we chat about the family, I say too much and, suddenly, we're talking about murder!"

"But that's what I'm here for, to talk about murder."

"Yes, but my tongue runs away with me and I find it difficult to realize that Matt is dead."

Wycliffe sat, unruffled in his chair, while Florrie calmed herself by going to make tea.

Soon she was back again and they were drinking tea and eating saffron cake.

"About the little hut—did Alfred and Maurice meet their girl-friends there?"

"Yes, but I don't think Alfred was much competition." She looked down at her hands. "I'm making it sound as though the little hut was some sort of brothel, but it wasn't like that at all. I mean, we were young; there happened to be more girls in the neighbourhood than boys, and we experimented—there was noth-ing vicious about it. Going back to Alfred, it was solemnly agreed that every couple who spent time in the hut would carve their initials somewhere. Of course it became quite a game searching for pairs of initials but I don't remember finding Alfred's once."

She cast a speculative eye on Lucy Lane. "Sometimes I get the impression that modern young people think they discovered sex."

"Did Sara come in on any of this?"

"Oh, no! Sara used to spy on the boys but if she ever had anything going for her I didn't know about it."

Lucy Lane said: "They all seemed fond of their mother."

Florrie smiled. "She was always a bit of a mystery to me; her sons worshipped her—I'm not so sure about Sara. If there was anything unpleasant the first thing in the boys' minds was 'not to worry Mother.' I've no idea how she managed it. Anyhow she lived to be nearly ninety and I'm not surprised."

They left at last. In the car Lucy Lane said: "A very interesting woman."

Wycliffe agreed. "A realist, and they're rare birds, God knows."

When they arrived back at the Incident Room the little printer was locking up for the night.

"Good evening, Mr. Wycliffe. Nice evening."

They were becoming neighbours.

Dixon, one of the longest serving of Wycliffe's DCs and one who had never sought or wanted promotion, was duty officer. "The chief's been on the line, sir; he wants you to ring him."

Dixon had been in the business long enough to convey by a subtle nuance of tone that the chief constable was not in an amiable mood.

"Right. Get him on the line; I'll be in my room."

His telephone rang almost at once; he was through to the chief's personal assistant, a grey-haired lady of vast experience who monitored and sometimes modulated communication (other than face to face) between the chief and the outside world—including his policemen.

"The chief's been asking for you for some time, Mr. Wycliffe." Her tone was caution.

"I've been out."

Bertram Oldroyd's voice came over the line. "Charles! Where the hell have you been? Never mind, you'll only tell me and I don't want to know. The press, the TV and the radio would like to know what's going on and, incidentally, so would I. Kersey doesn't know, or he does and isn't saying."

Wycliffe was wooden. "What exactly is it that is not known, sir? We've had a homicide and a suicide and your office has been kept informed about both."

Oldroyd laughed. "All right, Charles, come off it! You know damn well the questions that are being asked—the questions I'm asking: Is this case winding up or isn't it? The facts seem to point to Matthew Glynn having been murdered by his brother Alfred as the climax of a long feud aggravated by Alfred's mental instability. Alfred commits suicide which, in the circumstances, might well be construed as an admission of guilt. You've no reason to doubt the suicide?"

"None."

"Good! Then what are we waiting for?"

Wycliffe said: "There is another piece of evidence which hasn't reached you yet. The dead man's sister, Sara Glynn, has made a fresh statement in which she claims to have seen her brother Alfred leaving the scene shortly after the time at which Matthew must have died."

Oldroyd drew in his breath. "So that's it! Surely it's over bar the paperwork."

Wycliffe said: "I'm not satisfied, sir."

"What more do you want?"

"To be convinced."

There was a lull. Wycliffe could sense Oldroyd's mind ticking over. "All right, Charles. I've got too much respect for you to argue but I hope you'll remember that you're tying up men and equipment down there."

"I'll remember."

"How long do you reckon you'll need?"

"As long as it takes, sir."

"It's a good job I know you, Charles! Have it your way. I'll get Miller to draft a statement for the media and tell him to clear it with you before release."

"Thanks, I appreciate that."

That evening Wycliffe's after-dinner walk took him once more to Newlyn, but it was a fine evening and still light so he continued along the coast road, past the stone quarries, to Mousehole. (Nothing to do with mice or holes but probably a corruption of the Cornish *Moweshayl,* young women's river—perhaps where they did their washing.) He trudged the maze of little streets, sometimes on the edge of the sea, sometimes, and unpredictably, separated from it by a row of cottages. There was a quay, said to have been started by the Phoenicians; and everywhere, on sea and land alike, there were boats. Just another Cornish village in transition from fish to tourists.

He found Merlyn Rock where, in the summer of 1595, the Spaniards landed and burned the village along with Newlyn and Penzance; then in the gathering dusk he made his way up the hill out of the village to Paul and the church of St. Pol de Leon (not he of Tarsus but a Celtic gentleman), also burned by the Spaniards and rebuilt afterwards.

And all the time in the subterranean passages of his mind he was trying to come to terms with his own obstinacy. Why would Sara say that she had seen Alfred leaving his brother's yard at about the time of the crime if she had not? True, Alfred was not now in a position to contradict her, but why should she lie? To protect herself? To protect someone else? Either was possible but why did he disbelieve her? It came to him that what really troubled him was motive, or rather the lack of what he considered to be a convincing motive for the killing.

He reminded himself again that he was dealing with premeditated murder and the Glynns were not the sort to resort deliberately to force except in dire circumstances. They were respectable; they and their like inherit and sustain their respectability as the aristocracy guard the family silver—an ultimate resource.

He had taken a longer walk than he intended and by the time he returned to the coast road at Newlyn it was quite dark.

CHAPTER NINE

Wednesday morning

It was not yet May but it was a May morning; the sun was shining and there was that certain sparkle in the air; air which, despite all that has been done to it, Wycliffe still found good to breathe. And, according to the radio, doves were cooing in the Kremlin. He felt mildly exhilarated, which troubled him a little because he couldn't think why.

It was high tide and on the wharf the swing-bridge was open to allow a toy ship to enter the toy-town dry dock. He stood and watched for a while but everything connected with seamanship is so majestically slow that he began to feel guilty of time wasting while the little vessel was still being manoeuvred through the gap.

He climbed the steep slope to the Incident Room, forcing his pace, and arrived just a little out of breath. The printer had not yet opened.

Upstairs, Dixon, the duty officer, nodded towards the waiting-room. "A young lady to see you, sir—Christine Glynn."

She was sitting on one of the bentwood chairs, knees together, her hands wedged between them. She wore jeans and a zip-up denim top.

"You wanted to see me, Christine?"

Without a word she followed him into his office. He placed a chair for her and she sat down, pale and anxious.

"It's about when they opened Father's safe."

"You told me you weren't there."

"I wasn't; it was only when I was talking about it to Gina that I thought I ought to come here and tell you."

She was holding herself so stiff that from time to time she trembled. He tried to help her: "They didn't find much; only a couple of volumes of somebody's journal—"

"Yes, I know. And a box—an empty cardboard box."

"You know something about these things?"

"Only that I've seen them before."

"In the safe?"

"No."

"Tell me about it."

She frowned, making an effort to compose herself. "It was about a month ago; one afternoon I sort of burst into Father's office to ask him something. Paula said there was nobody with him but there was: Ronnie Swayne was there. Ronnie must have come in through the yard door without her knowing . . . Father hated to be disturbed when he had anybody with him and I could see he was annoyed so I made myself scarce; I mean I didn't stay to say what I wanted."

"But you saw something?"

"Yes. The safe was open, and the two books were on Father's desk with the cardboard box, and he was just taking the lid off the box as I came in."

"Was it empty?"

"No, it was full of papers."

"Papers lying on top of one another—just stuffed in?"

"No; they were sort of folded and put in next to each other, on edge."

"Like cards in a card index?"

She looked pleased. "Yes, just like that but they seemed too thick for cards and uneven—like folded papers. I can't say for sure; I mean, I was only there for a second or two . . ."

"Did your father say anything to you or to Swayne while you were there?"

"Not to me; I didn't stay long enough."

"To Swayne?"

"He was saying something as I came in—something about a buyer . . ."

"Having a buyer . . . finding a buyer . . . looking for a buyer . . . ?"

She shook her head. "I'm sorry, I can't remember."

He wondered why she was so tense. "Why have you come to tell me about this, Christine?"

"I thought you would want to know; I mean, there were things in the box that aren't there now."

She reminded him very much of his own daughter as she had been not so long ago; on the verge of womanhood, nervous and unsure but determined not to be put down or patronized.

"You think Swayne may have the things that were in the box?"

She drew back at this. "I don't know. Gina said that your . . . your detective seemed to think the box mattered. Perhaps I shouldn't have come."

He was reassuring. "You were quite right to come and what you've told me may be important. I just want to be sure that you've told me all you know."

He sat watching the girl, wondering if there was any way of getting behind the mask. She faced him, her dark eyes anxious.

"Do you believe that your Uncle Alfred killed your father?"

"Of course I believe it! Aunt Sara saw him—she told you!" Her response was so vigorous as to be almost violent.

He gave up. "Are you going out to the pottery today?"

"I'm on my way; I've got my bike outside."

He thanked her for coming and saw her off the premises, but he was left wondering at her distress which seemed to arise more from fear than from grief. But that did not prevent him seeing the possible significance of what she had told him.

Back in his office he put through a call to the colonel. After the obligatory preamble on the weather he got down to business. "When you were here you mentioned a collection of letters written by Martin Beale to his mother which came into your mother's possession later. How were they kept?"

"Kept?" The colonel echoed the word in his high-pitched voice. "In a shoe box or something of the sort. Don't tell me you've found them?"

"No, but we may have news of them. Were the letters loose or still in their envelopes?"

Hesitation. "I'm afraid I can't tell you that. My mother kept the box in a cupboard in her sitting-room along with all manner of other things which had been handed down through her side of the family. I remember her pointing it out to me saying what was in it when we were really looking for something else." The colonel pondered. "No, I don't think I ever looked inside. I suppose one gets more interested in that sort of thing as one grows older."

Wycliffe thanked him and promised to keep him informed.

Swayne; perhaps he should have paid more attention to Swayne.

Lady Street was busy: there were even a few visitors about, weaving between the parked vans and lorries. It's extraordinary the way they materialize like flies out of thin air when the sun shines. The grill had been removed from the window of the stamp shop and the outer door stood open. Wycliffe stepped down into the little hall and pushed open the door of the shop itself. There was a chest-high counter and the space on the customers' side offered room for no more than two people. Swayne, wearing his half-glasses, was seated on a high stool behind the counter, sorting stamps, dividing the contents of a large heap into several smaller piles. Clarence sprawled on the counter as only a cat can, performing an intimate and meticulous toilet.

Swayne looked over his glasses. "Good morning, Mr. Wycliffe. Do you want to come through?"

"No, this shouldn't take long."

Swayne went on: "I suppose it's about Alfred. A shocking business! One feels guilty about not having understood better what was going on. I'm assuming that it was suicide following . . ."

"Following what, Mr. Swayne?" Wycliffe was innocent.

"Well, one shouldn't jump to conclusions but I can't help linking Alfred's death with Matt's. I knew, of course—we all did—the bitterness which Alfred felt against his brother . . . But after nearly thirty years!"

Swayne's fingers continued busily sorting his stamps into colourful little heaps; he seemed to manage with the minimum of attention.

Wycliffe said: "It's not about Alfred that I'm here but another matter altogether. Among the contents of Matthew's safe there were two manuscript volumes, the journal of a certain Martin

Beale who lived and worked in Natal and Cape Province during the second half of the last century."

Swayne made no comment.

"I understand that Matthew showed you those books."

"Yes, he did."

"Do you know where he got them or why he kept them from his family?"

Swayne looked at Wycliffe over his glasses. "No, I don't know, Mr. Wycliffe. Surely you're not suggesting that they had anything to do with his death?"

"You didn't know that he acquired them through his wife who must have got them while she was housekeeper-companion to Mrs. Armitage?"

Swayne's fingers ceased sorting his stamps and he gave Wycliffe his full attention. "No, I didn't know that."

"In what circumstances were they shown to you?"

"Simply as a matter of interest. We happened to be talking about the diary habit which, nowadays, seems to be largely confined to politicians."

"Did he ask you to find a buyer for them?"

The little green eyes widened. "Mr. Wycliffe, Matthew was a dealer in rare books and something of an authority, why would he consult me?"

Wycliffe was standing with one arm resting on the counter, gazing at the freckled man whose sparse red hair was combed in streaks across his skull. For an appreciable time no one spoke and Swayne began to be uneasy. The cat had stopped cleaning itself and had curled up asleep in a little pool of sunshine.

Somebody stepped down from the street and peered through the glass door but seeing Wycliffe went away again.

Wycliffe said: "What about the letters?"

"The letters?"

"In the cardboard box; they were in the safe with the journal. Were you more interested in them? You see, they are no longer there."

Swayne fiddled with his little heaps of stamps. "Journals, letters —they were both Glynn's cup of tea, not mine."

"But letters come in envelopes and envelopes have stamps on

them. My mother always kept letters in their envelopes and a lot of other people must have done the same or the stamp business generally would have been the poorer."

"I'm at sea, Mr. Wycliffe."

"Then let me be more explicit. Inez had no right to either the journal or the box of letters which passed into Matthew Glynn's possession and were shown to you. Mrs. Armitage's heir is already asserting his rights in the matter but that is not my concern. My interest is in the murder of Matthew Glynn."

Swayne was incredulous. "But surely you know who killed Matthew?"

"No, I do not know! We have one possibility but the case is still under investigation and I am looking for possible motives. I don't know the value attaching to the stamps on those envelopes but if they are or have been in your possession you would be well advised to make a full statement of your involvement. If I can't get the information I want any other way I shall ask the fraud squad to make enquiries. At the same time you will be required to attend at the police station for a formal interview."

Swayne made an angry movement. "This is harassment!"

Wycliffe straightened up. "Of course if you wish to make a voluntary statement you can come along to my Incident Room at some time to suit yourself. One of the officers there will assist you." He left without giving the little man a chance to reply.

Out in the street he stood for a while, obstructing the pavement. Swayne was a dealer, it was doubtful whether he was making more than a bare living out of his stamps and coins. If there was a chance of real money he might be tempted . . . Assuming the cardboard box was full of letters and that each one carried a stamp—used stamps of Natal and Cape Province between the years say, 1850 and 1890—would they be worth much? Wycliffe had no idea but surely not enough to provide a motive for murder. All the same, he was in no doubt that Matthew Glynn had handed over the contents of the cardboard box to Swayne with a view to some sort of deal.

Give Swayne time to brood.

Without conscious intent he walked the few steps to the bookshop. The blinds were still down and there was a Closed notice on the door, but there was no longer a uniformed man outside. He rang the bell of the house door and it was answered by a grey-haired little woman in an overall; a Mrs. Mop. He had no need to introduce himself.

Brushing back her hair with the back of a damp hand she said: "Your lot are up in the attics, Miss Sara is out, and they're in the shop."

He went down the passage and through the communicating door into the shop. At the back he found Gerald and Paula, the girl assistant, unpacking parcels of books.

Gerald straightened up. "I was hoping you might put in an appearance. I know it sounds unfeeling but to be blunt we can't go on much longer without any money coming in. The coroner has issued a disposal certificate and we've provisionally arranged the funeral for Saturday—service at the church and burial in the town cemetery beside Granny." He looked at Wycliffe, oddly tentative. "Will the police raise any objection to that?"

"Why should we?"

"And we could open for business on Monday?"

"It's up to you."

The sound of a typewriter rattling away came from the little office and Gerald said: "Gina—catching up on the correspondence. She'd rather do it herself than dictate to Paula."

Gerald was uneasy, apologizing for the contending demands of the living and the dead, but Wycliffe was too preoccupied to be reassuring. "I'm going up to the attics."

He climbed the stairs, paused for a moment to look out of the landing window at the bay in sunshine, then continued on up. There were three attics and through the open door of one he could see Fox sorting the contents of a huge cabin-trunk while his assistant was foraging in a cupboard beside the chimney breast. The room had the steeply sloping ceiling and dormer window typical of attics.

There were heaps of clothing on the floor, roughly sorted and laid out on newspaper. Fox, house-trained and with a card-index mind, was shocked by the manner in which Inez's belongings had been stored.

"I gather Matthew Glynn put all this away himself. I've never seen such a jumble! There's a lot of very good stuff here but he seems to have gathered it up in armfuls and just bundled it in anywhere. When Leach opened that cupboard it just tumbled out on the floor."

He stooped to retrieve an ear-ring which had dropped out of a blouse he was holding. "Odd items of jewellery fall out of anything you happen to pick up; photographs are mixed up with under-clothes . . . Handbags over here, Leach!" He reached out to take a pigskin handbag from his assistant. "That's the fifth, so far—one to go with each outfit I suppose . . . That fur on the floor is mink . . . One thing's certain: he didn't keep her short . . ."

Wycliffe brooded; he felt restless and frustrated, unable to make up his mind where he should be or what he should be doing. And this attic depressed him; these expensive artefacts, stuffed away and unregarded, seemed to underline the futility of a certain kind of living . . . He tried to imagine Matthew's state of mind when he gathered up his wife's things and stashed them away. Glynn was not by nature careless or casual; he must have been under strong emotion. Grief? Anger? Remorse? . . .

"Look out particularly for any photographs or letters."

"There's an album with snapshots, sir, mainly of the children —'Gerry at five years,' 'Gina at four months'—that sort of thing."

Wycliffe was leaving when Leach lifted a bundle of clothing from the bottom shelf of his cupboard. "There's a brief-case under this lot!"

He stooped and held up a fairly modern brief-case of the sort office workers are said to carry their sandwiches in. Fox took it from him. "It's locked."

Wycliffe waited while Fox demonstrated his skill as a picklock. The case was all but empty—just a few letters, still in their enve-lopes.

"Three of them seem to be anonymous, sir," Fox said. "Ad-dressed in block capitals to Matthew Glynn."

Wycliffe took the three to a small table by the window. The envelopes had been slit open. All three had been posted in the Penzance district and the postmark dates were: February 1st, Feb-ruary 22nd, and March 21st, all in 1971. The last date was signifi-cant; it was the Monday following the Sunday on which Inez left home for the last time. Wycliffe read the notes in date order; each consisted of one or two lines of block capitals, written with a ballpoint.

The first read: "You know what's going on with your wife. What sort of man are you?" The second: "Most Sunday afternoons her car is in Badgers' Wood. You can see for yourself." And the third: "Her car was there on Sunday."

The other letters in the brief-case were a mixed bag and dated some time later. One was from an astrologer saying that he would find Matthew's wife for a fee; another proposed membership of a society for bereaved or deserted spouses; a third offered the services of "a well-known and respected private inquiry agent, formerly associated with Scotland Yard."

"I suppose neither of you have heard of Badgers' Wood?"

Neither of them had.

Outside the door he all but ran into Sara. Had she been eavesdropping? If so she had learned very little. He was astonished by the change in her since the previous day; then she had looked tired, now she looked grey and ill. Evidently the making of a formal statement had not relieved her mind.

"I heard you were up here going through what Inez left. Why? Surely you can leave us alone now?" Her manner was pleading rather than aggressive.

"I have to do my work, Miss Glynn." Smug; but what else could he say?

"What work? You know who killed Matthew—and why. What more do you want, for God's sake?"

He could not be touched by this woman though he was well aware that she was deeply distressed. "I'm sorry."

She let him go without further protest.

His mind was in turmoil. He wanted to get away somewhere and think in peace, but experience had taught him that it would have achieved nothing because he was incapable of sustained logical thought. The best he could hope for was to give his thoughts free rein, to recapture phrases, images, notions, and play with them, allowing them to make patterns in his mind. While reading the anonymous notes the glimmering of an idea had come to him but he could not sharpen the focus. It was like trying to recall a dream.

Without being aware of getting there he found himself outside the printer's shop. Upstairs, Curnow was duty officer.

"I want a driver and the key to the little hut at Trebyan."

He got one of the local uniformed men.

"Trebyan—beyond St. Hilary Churchtown."

"I know it, sir."

"You know the area well?"

"I ought to, I was born and bred in Penzance; PC Hawken, sir."

Late thirties, ought to have made sergeant by now but probably didn't want to. Who could blame him?

"Have you ever heard of Badgers' Wood?"

"No, sir. There's Badgers' Cross—"

"I know Badgers' Cross."

They turned off the main road. "Take the lane to Churchtown."

"There's no need, sir, this road will—"

"Do it."

If PC Hawken had heard of Wycliffe's reputation for amiability he was being disillusioned.

"Stop here."

There was no dog in the road but they were among the little cluster of grey and brown stone houses near the church where Wycliffe had had his memorable conversation with Emily Pascoe.

He went to her house and knocked on the green door. It was answered by Emily herself, an oven cloth in her hand.

"Oh, it's you! Come in, do!"

He was shown into an over-furnished little sitting-room from which the light was almost excluded by two sets of curtains. A rich warm smell of baking came from the kitchen.

"I just this minute took my cakes out of the oven. I always bake of a Wednesday, just like my mother used to—two saffron cakes and a tray of buns—they last us nicely through the week." She made a gesture of vigorous distaste. "I can't abide they ol' shop cakes."

She guided him to an armchair and sat herself on the edge of a Victorian sofa. "What a terrible thing about poor Alfie! You could've knocked me down with a feather when they tol' me." She studied her plump, ringed fingers. "I come over quite queer. To

think that was what the poor fella was going to do when I saw 'n
pass my door Monday morning!''

"Yes, it was a terrible thing. I came this morning because I think
you may be able to help me from your knowledge of the family
and of the area. First, do you know a place called Badgers' Wood?''

She frowned. "Badgers' Wood? . . . No, I never heard that
name round here an' I've lived here all my life . . . Badgers'
Wood—no, I can't help you there, my dear. 'Course, there's badgers up in the banks but I never heard that name—'' She broke
off. "You was saying about the family . . .''

"Yes. I wanted to ask you about Maurice's wife—you mentioned
her when—''

"Yes, she come from somewhere up-country. Poor li'l thing, she
didn' last long. Depression. In an' out of hospital she was.'' She
gave Wycliffe a sidelong look. "They call it hospital now—what we
used to call the asylum. She never got over having young David—
sad! But like I said before, they Glynns never had much luck.''

"In the end she couldn' stand it no longer.''

"Are you saying that she killed herself?''

Emily pouted her lips. "Overdose. Funny! Not one of they
brothers got and kept a wife.''

Through a narrow gap in the curtains Wycliffe could see across
the road to the churchyard with its sycamores and the little grey
tower of the church pointing its slender steeple into blue sky. Not
a movement, not a sound anywhere.

"Did Maurice have any help in the house when his wife was in
hospital?''

"Molly Pearce. She was good as gold; I don't know what he
would've done without her!''

"An elderly woman?''

"Elderly? Nothing of the kind—thirtyish I s'pose she must've
bin then.'' A knowing smile. "I reckon she had her eye on Maurice when his wife died.''

"I'd like to talk to her; does she still live around here?''

"Where she always lived; she never married.''

"Where is that?''

"With her people—they farm Roskear; it's on the top road just
above Trebyan. The Glynns and the Pearces are neighbours.''

Wycliffe came out into the sunshine, blinking; Emily saw him off like an old friend. She would probably gossip; so much the better.

PC Hawken was waiting in the car.

Wycliffe made up his mind: "I shall be at Trebyan for a while."

"Then I'll drop you off there, sir."

"No, I prefer to walk. Are you interested in churches?"

"I can take them or leave them, sir."

"Never been in this one?"

"No, sir."

"Try it. Pity there's no pub."

After twenty years in the force Hawken thought that he knew all there was to be known about the eccentricities of senior officers but he was wrong.

Wycliffe set out along the road which was no more than a lane following the course of a shallow valley. There were fields on either side with occasional stands of pine trees scattered unpredictably over the landscape. In the hedges bluebells, red campions and white ramsons made patriotic splashes of colour.

Not a single vehicle.

Molly Pearce, the helpful spinster with her eye on Maurice; she fitted so exactly that Wycliffe could scarcely believe his luck. He was beginning to find pieces which seemed to go together with the hint of a pattern . . .

Strolling rather than walking he reached the point where the footpath to Trebyan left the road; it was by no means obvious unless one was looking for it: a ditch, a screen of willows, and a stile all but covered with ivy. Once over the stile he was soon amongst the hawthorn and gorse and on the track which led to the little hut; he was doing as Alfred must have done two days earlier.

It was a strange place and it gave him strange ideas; he was oddly aware of those who had played, and loved, and quarrelled there. Had they done so with more than ordinary intensity so that they had left behind something of themselves—a persistent aura? He told himself that this was nonsense; he was allowing his knowledge to influence his perceptions.

Yet Alfred had chosen it as a place to die and David had said of his father: ". . . for him it is one of those special places."

He reached the hut and climbed the two or three steps to the verandah. The silence was absolute; the sun shone and the air was still. Then he noticed that there was a key already in the lock. He opened the door but the dimness inside was such that for a moment he could see little; then, as his eyes accommodated, he saw Maurice standing, pressed against the far wall as though he wanted to vanish through it. The hut seemed to be as he had last seen it except that the settee had been pulled out from the wall to the centre of the room.

In a voice that sounded husky and uncertain, Maurice said: "I came down to look around."

"So you found another key."

CHAPTER TEN

Wednesday morning (continued)

Wycliffe sat on the settee in the middle of the room; Maurice was perched on the stool, hands and knees tight together as though, absurdly, he would make himself as small as possible.

"I suppose you know that your sister made a fresh statement yesterday?"

"She told me—on the telephone."

"According to her statement she saw Alfred leaving the Lady Street premises by the back door at about half-past eleven on Saturday night."

"I know."

Their attitudes were not those of two men meeting for only the second time; it was rather as if they shared certain knowledge and could make a number of assumptions which need not be stated. For all that, the atmosphere was tense.

"You believed what Sara told you?"

"Why would she lie?"

"In two previous interviews she made contradictory assertions."

"That was before Alfred committed suicide. You could hardly expect her to deliberately incriminate him." Maurice produced his pipe from the pocket of his denim jacket and held it up in an unsteady hand. "Do you mind?"

"Carry on. What Sara did would be equally explicable if she saw it as safe to accuse Alfred when he was no longer in a position to defend himself."

Maurice was making a tremendous effort to appear calm but there was tension in his every movement. In the act of filling his pipe he was hampered by trembling hands which he tried in vain to steady by pressing them against his thighs.

"I don't understand. Why should she say she saw Alfred if she didn't see him?"

"To protect someone else? Herself, perhaps?"

"You think that Sara killed Matthew?" His manner was incredulous.

"What do you think?"

He put the stem of his pipe in his mouth, gripped it hard, and spoke through his teeth. "I believe Sara—implicitly."

Wycliffe seemed to relax. For some time they sat in silence and Maurice went through the ritual of lighting his pipe and persuading it to draw. The sun shone directly through the little window panes creating a broad path of light which divided the hut into two and cast strong shadows on the opposite wall.

Pinned to that wall there was a 1:25,000 Ordnance map of the immediate area. Wycliffe got up from the settee to examine it. The map was annotated in pencil with sightings of birds and other animals. After an interval he said: "I don't see Badgers' Wood marked on this map."

For a long moment there was no response then Maurice said: "Badgers' Wood?"

"Never mind; perhaps Florrie Tremayne will remember."

Maurice forced a laugh. "It was a name we invented as kids. God knows where you got it from. Have you been talking to Florrie? We used to play the sort of games kids did then: Robin Hood, cowboys and Indians, war games . . ." he was talking to stave off the next question. "We were lucky, we had this hut and the free run of the country around as long as we didn't tread on the crops or forget to shut gates. Like kids do, we had our own names for bits of the countryside—"

"And Badgers' Wood?"

Maurice got up from his stool and came over to the map. With the stem of his pipe he pointed to a small area of green behind Trebyan, close to another country road which eventually converged with the one running past Trebyan. "That was the place we called Badgers' Wood; it's a little cluster of pines; I doubt if anybody ever saw any badgers there."

Within a short distance of the wood the map showed a group of buildings labelled Roskear.

"Did Molly Pearce join in these games?"

Another interval before Maurice said in a tired voice: "Molly Pearce? It's a long time ago but I expect so; most of the kids about here did."

"And later, after you were married, she came to look after you and David when your wife was in hospital?"

Maurice turned to face him, his expression both puzzled and concerned. He said: "Yes, she did. Molly was very good, but what—?"

"I understand that your wife died of an overdose, Mr. Glynn?"

"Yes . . . She was receiving treatment for depression, in and out of hospital."

"She wasn't in hospital at the time of her death?"

"No, she was at home."

"That was some time after your sister-in-law, Inez, disappeared?"

"Inez went away in March and Celia died in January of the following year—1972. I really can't understand why you are asking me all this!"

Wycliffe was cool. "Don't disturb yourself, I am trying to get some perspective on the events. Was there an inquest on your wife?"

"Yes; and the verdict was suicide while the balance of her mind was disturbed."

"Of what drug did she take an overdose?"

"Phenobarbitone."

"Prescribed for depression?"

Maurice's reply was barely audible. "No, it was prescribed for me; I was suffering from stress—it was a difficult time."

Wycliffe nodded. He seemed to have lost interest in the questioning and he was looking around the hut with apparently casual interest. Abruptly, he said: "Why did you shift the settee, Mr. Glynn?"

"I dropped something down the back."

"I was under the impression that we held the only key. I would prefer that you do not make use of the hut until our enquiries are complete."

"But I don't understand—"

"You object?"

"No, I don't object."

"Then perhaps you will let me keep both keys for the time being. I don't want to go to the length of putting seals on the door and making the whole thing much more official."

It was odd. Wycliffe's words were reasonable enough and he did not raise his voice or give them any particular emphasis, yet there was an element of menace.

He got up from the settee and stood by the open door for a dazed Maurice to pass through. Outside, he locked the door and pocketed the key. "I shall be coming again; in the meantime I may send someone to take a closer look at things in the hut."

He glanced at his watch; it was half-past one.

Striving to sound normal, Maurice said: "David will be wondering where I am."

As he came down the verandah steps Wycliffe spotted David hurrying away up the path towards the house. Had the boy been listening? What did it matter? Wycliffe went down the slope towards the road.

He felt like the fly-fisherman who makes his cast, draws his lure through the water, hooks his fish, then "plays" it until the poor creature surrenders. Wycliffe was far from that stage but he had no stomach for the role; inflicting suffering of any kind, especially on the innocent, was repugnant to him. But if you are a policeman, a politician, a businessman, a trade unionist or even a human being, you have to believe that in some degree the end justifies the means.

Hawken was waiting for him in the car. "I had a look in the church, sir."

"Well?"

"I liked the pictures, especially the ones painted by the little girl."

"Are you expected home for lunch?"

"No, sir; it's canteen grub for me today."

"Then let's find a pub where we can get something to eat."

Wycliffe arrived back at the Incident Room shortly before three. Fox, the scenes-of-crime officer, was there.

"In the morning I want you and a couple of DCs at Trebyan."

"What will we be doing there, sir?"

"I'll brief you in the morning."

"We could make a start now, sir; there are several hours of daylight left."

"In the morning."

He was standing in the main room, brooding. There were only two DCs and Lucy tapping away at their word processors. The inquiry had started on a small scale, now it was dying for want of what it fed upon. Statements had been checked and rechecked; everybody in the neighbourhood had been questioned at least once; and most of this was to protect one's rear. A sufficient bulk of paper in the form of reports or computer printouts is the only material evidence that stones have been turned, avenues explored, and the fine-toothed comb diligently employed.

But from the start Wycliffe had been convinced that this crime would prove to concern a small group of people who were closely, even intimately connected. Nowadays so many major crimes are wide open and impersonal: A kills, or rapes, or mugs B, but X, Y, or Z would have done just as well. The only hope of catching A is to field a large team, accumulate vast quantities of data, and make full use of the almost infinite collating resources of the computer. But in this case, what would he do with a large team? And what use was the computer except as a substitute for the old carousel— a convenient memory jogger?

He muttered to himself: "By now Sara will have heard all about it."

Lucy Lane looked up from her machine. "Sir?"

"Nothing."

A familiar voice at the duty officer's desk made him look in that direction. "Take Mr. Swayne to my office."

He said to Lucy Lane: "I want you in on this."

Swayne was nervous, like a mouse who is doubtful about what goes with the cheese. He was seated in the client's chair with a small suitcase on his lap. His little red fingers beat a silent tattoo.

Wycliffe sat opposite him and Lucy Lane took a chair by the door. Swayne opened his case and took out a package and a stout envelope. He pointed to the package. "The letters, still in their envelopes, as they were in the cardboard box you spoke of. There are a hundred and fifty of them, all from Beale to his mother, and they date between 1850 and 1890. The stamps on them are of interest and have some value but they won't make anybody's fortune."

"What about the envelope?"

Swayne touched the envelope almost with reverence. "That is a different matter. You see, Beale, in a letter to his mother in the very early sixties, said that he had heard of the new hobby of collecting stamps and that he would send home some from time to time which she could give to his nephews in case they were interested." Swayne could not keep the enthusiasm out of his voice.

"From then on he included with almost every letter a number of stamps, the great majority in mint condition, many with rare overprintings and surcharges, some—by chance—with printing or design faults, retouches, et cetera . . . Well, for some reason, his mother did not pass on the stamps to his nephews, she left them in the envelopes in which they had come."

"And you were supposed to sell them on Glynn's behalf through one of the auction houses?"

The bubble of Swayne's enthusiasm was pricked. "Well, not exactly—"

"No! Because of their questionable provenance it had to be an under-the-counter deal. But are you sure that you intended to sell them at all? Who knew that you had them other than Glynn himself? And Glynn is dead."

"Mr. Wycliffe! I am—"

"I know—I know! You are a reputable dealer, but you were willing to undertake this dubious bit of business for a friend. Unfortunately your friend was murdered, and it has taken you three days and some pressure to admit to possession of the letters and the stamps."

"I would have approached the family—"

Wycliffe made a dismissive gesture; he sounded bored. "Yes, of course! At a more appropriate time—after the funeral, when they have had time to settle down—this year, next year, sometime, never . . . Put it in your statement, Mr. Swayne. I presume that you came here to make one? Detective Sergeant Lane will take you into the next room and arrange it."

Swayne's apprehensive green eyes looked at him over the half-glasses, "But what happens then?"

"I've no idea."

"At least you are satisfied now that I had nothing to do with what happened to poor Matt?"

Wycliffe shrugged. "I don't think you are a murderer, Mr. Swayne; perhaps you are not a rogue, but I think you contemplated becoming one."

Pressure was building; Swayne had already yielded up his morsel of the truth. To be effective, applying psychological pressure must be a gradual process, a slow build-up so that the subjects have time to think, to reflect, and convince themselves that they are grist for the mills of God.

In the absence of material evidence it may be the only way, but to use it requires a thorough knowledge of the subjects, their backgrounds, their strengths, their loyalties, their weaknesses, and their fears. Especially their fears . . .

"In my experience fear is the most powerful drive to violence among such people, but why should any of them in this case be afraid?"

His own words, and he silently endorsed them now. The position was unchanged, the questions remained: who was afraid, and of what? Perhaps, of the two, "of what?" was the more important now.

Nit-picking by telephone from headquarters occupied him for the better part of an hour: the police lawyer worrying away at the fine detail of a case in preparation for the DPP; Wycliffe's personal assistant, the unflappable and impregnable Diane, on queries from Accounts about DCs' overtime and expenses; his deputy, John Scales, about reports for a forthcoming promotions board and a possible date for a crime prevention seminar.

They were ganging up on him, and by the time it was over he had mentally lost touch with the Glynns and their bookshop, with Trebyan, the pottery, and the little hut. He wanted to get back; he collected his car from outside the Incident Room and with a sense of release, he drove up Lady Street and down Market Jew—the main shopping street. (No connection with the chosen people, the name comes from the Cornish *Marghas Yow,* Thursday Market.)

He intended to approach Trebyan by a different route, by the top road which would take him past Badgers' Wood, and Roskear where Molly Pearce lived with her family. On the Ordnance map he had noticed a footpath leading from the top road, through Badgers' Wood and the fields above Trebyan, down through the scrub to the lower road.

Five minutes after leaving the A394 he thought he was lost but St. Michael, patron saint of coppers, had an eye on him. A few minutes more and he came upon a little cottage by a clump of pines and, a few yards farther on, a house with a cluster of farm buildings, and a gate labelled Roskear Farm.

It was not possible to turn the car in the narrow lane so he reversed back to the pines and the cottage. Badgers' Wood? The pines were not fenced off from the road; there was a way in, a beaten track through the trees wide enough for a vehicle, but Wycliffe left his car and walked.

He did not like pine woods, they reminded him of Jack London's Klondyke: frozen snow, howling wolves, and frostbite. Pines, he thought, needed the redeeming Mediterranean sun; here the late-afternoon April sunshine filtered through the branches but without warmth.

The track led to a small clearing. "Most Sunday afternoons her car is in Badgers' Wood." This, according to Matthew Glynn's anonymous correspondent. There would have been plenty of room for the little red Mini, hidden from the road.

A narrower version of the track continued on the other side of the clearing and he followed it to the far edge of the wood where he was faced by a hedge and a stile. Standing on top of the stile he could see across a couple of fields to Trebyan, the house and the buildings around the yard. Presumably it was by this route that Inez kept her trysts; hiding her car, trekking across muddy fields . . . What possessed a mature woman with a family and a secure home to indulge in these adolescent games? It was very odd, and he was intrigued.

The first field was in grass, with cows grazing; the second, which seemed smaller, looked like a market garden, almost certainly part of the Trebyan domain.

Wycliffe set out across the fields. There was no discernible path but at the other end of the first field there was another stile. Like so many field paths this one had fallen into disuse. The second stile took him into a very small field laid out like a garden, with areas set aside for potatoes, cabbages, root vegetables, and beans . . . Here there were grassy paths between the beds.

The stile at the end of this field led, not to the house and yard, but into the scrub of gorse and hawthorn. From the top of the stile he could see the roof of the little hut but the path beyond the stile was so overgrown as to be impassable. Obviously it had once served as a shortcut for people living along the top road on their way to St. Hilary church or to the school. For Inez it was her way to the little hut.

From where he stood he could look down into the backyard of Trebyan. A man came out from the house carrying a large wicker basket and went to a shed in the yard. It was Maurice. A minute or two later he returned with the basket full of small logs. Wycliffe willed him to look up and just as he was about to re-enter the house he turned, and did so. The distance was too great for Wycliffe to see his expression but the hesitation was obvious. Finally, with a nervous wave, he went inside and shut the door behind him. Wycliffe, satisfied, returned to the road.

He walked along to Roskear. The farmhouse was trim and colourful—pale pink walls and white paintwork—and it stood in its own garden, quite separate from the farmyard. In the yard twenty-five or thirty black-and-white Friesians were penned for milking and Wycliffe could hear the whirr of the machine. He rang the doorbell and it was answered by a middle-aged woman, tall and very fair.

"Miss Pearce? Miss Molly Pearce? . . . Chief Superintendent Wycliffe." He produced his warrant card.

She was an attractive woman: an oval face with good features, a mass of fair hair, and blue eyes with long lashes, but he was most impressed by the serenity of her expression.

"If I could come inside . . ."

He was shown into the parlour, a large comfortable room, obviously much used, by no means dirty but not overzealously cleaned. There was a piano, a television, a rack overflowing with farming papers and magazines, and a set of well-worn leather-upholstered armchairs. There were three or four coloured prints on the walls, but framed photographs of farming occasions predominated.

She removed newspapers from a chair. "Do sit down." The only words she had actually spoken so far.

"I'm sure you will have heard about the murder of Matthew Glynn and the death of his brother Alfred."

"Yes."

"I understand that you have known the Glynn family all your life."

She did not bother to answer that.

A black-and-white border collie padded into the room, sniffed around Wycliffe then settled on the hearthrug with an eye on him still.

"Mr. Maurice Glynn told me that when his wife became ill after the birth of their son you helped him a great deal in looking after the house and the baby."

He was finding it hard going. She sat opposite him, calmly attentive, her eyes unwavering in their gaze. "His sister, Sara, and I helped out where we could."

"We have reason to think that the events of the past week are linked to what happened at and around that time . . ."

He was being forced to ask direct questions which he had wanted to avoid.

"I suppose you knew Inez Glynn?"

"Yes, I knew her."

"Was she a regular visitor at Trebyan?"

"She was quite friendly with Celia—Maurice's wife."

"Have you ever heard of Badgers' Wood, Miss Pearce?"

The first tremor of disquiet; she hesitated. At that moment there were heavy footsteps in the passage and the door was pushed open. A big man stood in the doorway; brown jerkin and trousers, sandy hair, an amiable teddy bear of a man. "Oh, there you are, Moll! I didn't know . . . Sorry! Dad's fussing because he can't find the milk book."

"It's on the desk in the office. I saw it there ten minutes ago."

"Oh, good! Sorry, but you know what he's getting like . . ."

The door closed again and Wycliffe said, softly: "Badgers' Wood . . ."

She had recovered her poise. "It comes from when we were children; the name we local kids gave to the little pine wood along the road."

"From where there was a footpath to Trebyan and the little hut."

She assented by a slight movement of her head. Even now she had sufficient restraint neither to comment nor ask questions.

Wycliffe went on: "We have anonymous notes written to Matthew Glynn just before Inez disappeared telling him of her car being parked in Badgers' Wood on Sundays. I understand that at that time Maurice's wife was in hospital."

"What has this to do with me?"

"As you were helping out at Trebyan at that time and you would, presumably, have used the footpath to get to and from the place, it seems likely you would know something about it."

She seemed to come to some decision. "Mr. Wycliffe, you are asking me to recall things that happened many years ago. All I can say is that I never saw Inez in Maurice Glynn's house when his wife was not there. I imagine that Maurice will have a clearer recollection of what happened at that time."

Wycliffe had to settle for that. He drove back through the lanes, thinking not of Maurice nor of Molly Pearce, but of Inez. From an unpromising springboard, housekeeper-companion to an old lady, she had laid siege to Alfred Glynn, a young man at the start of his career as a pharmacist with his own business. While their conjugal bed was still in the making she had become pregnant by Alfred's brother Matthew. By the time her child was born she was the wife of the bookseller, while Alfred was left to turn his misfortune into a tragedy and begin constructing the fantasy which had apparently sustained him until the last few days.

It seemed that eleven years of marriage and three children had done nothing to abate Inez's taste for variety. In addition to certain nebulous exogamous relationships it now appeared that she had rounded off her Penzance period in the little hut, in Maurice's arms if not his bed; Maurice, the third and youngest of the Glynns. And this, according to the anonymous letters, was known to her husband.

So, the sixty-four dollar question: Had Inez gone off to explore new territory or had her career been brought to a dramatic end on that last Sunday?

In a letter posted the day after her disappearance Matthew's anonymous correspondent had said: "Her car was there on Sunday."

Wycliffe was back on the A394 and heading for the town. Time to forget about Inez; perhaps time to remind himself that all this had happened seventeen years ago; that it was only days since Matthew Glynn's murder, two days since Alfred's suicide. Was he chasing shadows?

But it was only four months since the three brothers had lost their mother; the final severance of the silver cord.

Plenty of questions but few answers and no obvious way of getting more.

He found Kersey in the hotel bar and they went into the dining-room together.

When they had ordered, Kersey said: "Angela Bickers: fifty-two or -three, good-looking woman, on the plump side, a sense of humour, and contented." A wry grin. "Not many of them about."

"She doesn't sound like a friend of Inez."

"She was though. At the time Inez went missing Angela and her husband were living in Hayle; her husband was a rep for something or other and away a lot so the two women used to see a good deal of each other. Attraction of opposites according to Angela. She talked a lot, but the gist of it was that though Inez was fed to the back teeth with Matthew and Sara, she had no intention of leaving her children."

"A pity she didn't say that to the police when Inez went missing."

"She wanted to but her husband insisted she should keep out of it. He didn't like her associating with Inez anyway—a woman who slept around. Thought it might be catching, I expect."

"So she admitted that Inez slept around?"

"Oh, she made no secret of the fact."

"Did she know that Inez was having an affair with Maurice?"

"She not only knew, she acted as go-between. I fancy she got her kicks that way. At that time Celia, Maurice's wife, was in and out of hospital for treatment; she'd be in for a few days then, perhaps, home for the weekend, depending on how she was.

"Maurice and Inez had their trysts on Sundays when Inez was supposed to be visiting her girlfriend. If Celia was coming home that weekend Maurice would let Angela know and she would pass the message on: 'Afraid I shan't be in Sunday—see you next week.' "

Kersey was tucking in to roast lamb while Wycliffe toyed with a prawn salad, his appetite still jaded by his lunchtime pasty. The dining-room was fuller than they had seen it so far; in addition to the usual sprinkling of up-market reps and businessmen, there were two or three family groups and an obvious honeymoon couple, like the cuckoo and the primrose, harbingers of summer.

Wycliffe asked: "Did she ever leave a message with another member of the family?"

Kersey grinned. "I asked her that. She did. Why shouldn't she? The message would sound innocent enough."

"With Matthew?"

"Sometimes—yes."

The two men ate in silence for a while then Kersey said: "What's the programme for tomorrow?"

"I've arranged for Fox and his team to be at Trebyan. We'll go to work on the hut."

"Expecting?"

"I'll tell you if we find it." Wycliffe finished his salad, sipped his wine and patted his lips. "Now, these people who've been checking on how Maurice spent Saturday evening—any joy?"

"Not so far; not a whisper. You're pretty sure he's our man, sir?"

"I'm by no means sure that Maurice killed his brother; even if I was, we haven't enough evidence to arrest a cat."

When they reached the coffee stage Kersey said: "Going for your walk, sir?"

"No, I'm going to talk to Sara."

He walked along the promenade in the darkness; there was a

fresh breeze off the sea, the lights of Marazion twinkled through a sea mist and there was salt on his lips. Although it was by no means rough he was more than ordinarily aware of the vast expanse of dark water and of the seemingly fragile margins of the land so that it appeared almost a miracle that the land was not overwhelmed.

By contrast the narrow confines of Lady Street were cloistered and secure. He walked up past Alfred's pharmacy. After only four days the street had become home ground. There were lights in the rooms above many of the shops and the shops were interspersed with ordinary houses. Wycliffe liked that; he felt instinctively that something went wrong when the planners started thinking in terms of "zones," a damning word anyway when associated with human activities.

Arrived at the Glynn house, he rang the doorbell and it was answered by Gina.

"Aunt Sara? She's up in her room; I'll tell her you're here."

"No, I'll go up." It was a spur-of-the-moment decision.

She looked at him in surprise but said nothing.

"Which room?"

"Turn right at the top of the stairs and it's the second door."

He tapped on the door and a voice called: "Come in!"

She was sitting in an armchair by a gas fire, she wore heavily rimmed reading glasses and she had a book in her hands; a table lamp by her chair cast a circle of light which left most of the room in darkness.

She looked up at him in total astonishment. "By what right—"

"I wanted a private word with you." His manner was placatory.

Sara was disposed to aggression but caution prevailed. She was angry but she was also scared. "Very well, now you are here you had better sit down."

She got up and switched on the main light so that the room came to life. To his surprise it was attractive, well furnished, and functional; the in-college room of a well-heeled spinster don: a couple of armchairs and a couch, upholstered in Liberty fabric; curtains out of the same stable; a large carpet square of Persian design, perhaps of Persian origin; a business-like mahogany desk and bookshelves. On the walls there were five or six modern woodcuts of an enigmatic genre. No photograph of Mother.

He did not sit down but stood looking at her books: a wide selection of modern fiction, a shelf or two of the classics, another of poetry, and a substantial collection of books on Cornwall including a number of language texts in a section to themselves.

"You read Cornish, Miss Glynn?"

"With difficulty and a dictionary." Snappish. She was predictably unforthcoming and impatient. "What exactly do you want with me, Mr. Wycliffe? Last Saturday I had three brothers, Matthew, Alfred, and Maurice. That night Alfred, sadly disturbed in his mind, attacked and killed Matthew. Two days later, in a fit of remorse, he committed suicide in a manner that is too terrible to think of." She paused and looked him in the eyes: "Surely we deserve some sympathy and understanding even from the police. Now that you know what happened, why do you continue to harass us?"

He was conciliatory. "I do understand, Miss Glynn, but in a police inquiry it is not sufficient to be able to say: "Here is the culprit." One has to present the background and the reasoning which makes that conclusion not only credible, but compelling." He broke off to settle himself in one of the armchairs, then waffled comfortably on: "You tell me that the motive for your brother's murder is to be found in events which happened a long time ago: I have to be clear what those events were, who was involved, and the nature of their involvement. I must also look at other possibilities."

Sara's manner was still suspicious and inclined to aggression but she was mollified. "So?"

"So, how can I get such information except from the people most intimately concerned? Any other source is likely to be no better than gossip. I hope you understand that, Miss Glynn?"

"And if I do, what do you want to ask me?"

"I would rather that we avoided specific questions; it would be more helpful if you were prepared to talk freely about your family and about the events which might have led to these tragedies at this time."

It was a smoke screen of words but it made a kind of sense and might encourage her to drop her guard.

With exaggerated patience she said: "Very well; what do you want to talk about?"

He said nothing for a while. A carriage clock on the mantelpiece ticked audibly through the silence. It was ten minutes past nine. When he spoke his words came as an anticlimax: "You can't have found life easy during those years when you shared this house with your sister-in-law."

A quick look to judge his motive for the remark, but there was little to be learned from his expression of bland interest. In the end she said: "I have never found life particularly easy, Mr. Wycliffe, but I have always been able to cope." She added after a pause: "I would certainly never have allowed my brother or his wife to drive me from my home."

Wycliffe said nothing. If an expected response is withheld and the silence is allowed to lengthen, the chances are that the other party will feel compelled to bridge the gap. It worked with Sara: "If I accepted the traditional role of an unmarried Glynn woman it was because I chose to. As far as Matthew was concerned he couldn't do without me either before or after his wife left him—and he knew it."

In a significant glance Wycliffe took in the room, which compared very favourably with anything he had seen in the rest of the house. "So that you were able to stay on your own terms."

She said nothing and the ball was back in Wycliffe's court.

"Both of your brothers seemed to have had grievances against Matthew. Was he a very difficult man?"

She considered how far she might go on this and decided to plunge. "Matthew was spoiled by Father; he was the only one of the sons who fitted Father's idea of what a son should be, and want, and do." She broke off, having become more animated than he had yet seen her and, perhaps for the first time, her words seemed to come from the heart: "Maurice was abominably treated in my father's will, and Matthew exploited the situation." She broke off with an irritable movement. "But you know that already."

In a low voice Wycliffe said: "And Alfred? What about Alfred?"

She stopped to think before saying: "Well, you know what happened to Alfred, that is what this is all about."

"And what was your father's attitude when Matthew took Inez from his brother? Or were you too young to understand much about it?"

"Of course I understood what was happening! I was eighteen! Father's attitude was indulgent towards Matthew and contemptuous of Alfred. I remember him saying to Mother: 'Alfred will never run a successful business or keep a woman.' "

The silence in the room was complete so that a casual exchange between two passers-by in the street reached them with startling clarity. Sara had spoken with an uncharacteristic lack of restraint, even with excitement, and Wycliffe wondered whether he could lead her farther along the same path.

Very quietly, he said: "And what was your mother's attitude to her three sons?"

Sara shifted in her chair, rearranging her skirt in a way that had become familiar to him when she was playing for time. He expected that she would evade the question or offer a conventional response; instead she was devastatingly objective.

"It is not the sort of thing one should say about a recently dead parent but my mother flirted with her sons." Sara's hands were clasped tightly in her lap and she was looking down at them. "Mother distributed her favours in such a way as deliberately to create jealousies, then she would chide them, playing with them like a . . . like a . . ." Her voice faltered and she broke off. She looked up and Wycliffe was astonished to see her eyes glistening with tears.

"Just one or two more questions, Miss Glynn. Do you remember clearly the Sunday morning your sister-in-law left home for the last time?"

"I remember it very well."

"Was your brother Matthew at home when his wife left?"

"No, at that time Matt took long walks of a Sunday; he would go off in the morning and come back in the afternoon having had a snack lunch in one of the pubs on his route."

"Was young David with you that weekend?"

She looked at him in surprise. "So you know about that. We

always had him here when his mother was coming home. It was one of the strange features of her illness that she couldn't bear to see her child."

"Did he stay long?"

"Several days—it gave Maurice a chance to catch up on his work at the pottery."

Wycliffe walked back to his hotel hardly aware of his route. For once he walked beside the sea at night without being impressed or even aware. He was thinking of Sara. She had given him more than he had expected, more than he had hoped, but she remained an enigmatic figure at the very core of his case. He had made a decision based more on an intuitive feel for the way people behave than on evidence, and he was staking his credibility on that decision.

CHAPTER ELEVEN

Thursday morning

Wycliffe was awakened by Kersey tapping on his bedroom door. Kersey in his dressing gown stood by the bed, just visible in the thin, pale light which found its way through the window curtains.

"The duty officer chickened out from disturbing you and asked for me instead. The hut at Trebyan is on fire; the brigade is attending but it's unlikely they can do much. The fire was reported by a patrol car crew and, knowing our interest, the duty officer thought he ought to tell somebody."

Wycliffe had been engaged in a frantic search for his parked car in a Kafkaesque town where streets, with no names, were all alike and the inhabitants appeared to be both deaf and dumb. For some moments at least reality was a relief from the dream.

He looked at his travelling clock; it was 5:37.

"I suppose we'd better get out there."

"I don't see there's much we can do until they get the fire out."

"We can try to find out who set it alight."

"Surely that's obvious, it can only have been Maurice."

Wycliffe was getting out of bed. "Would he be such a fool?"

They scrounged coffee and rolls through the night porter and by soon after six they were on their way in Wycliffe's car with Kersey driving.

As they drove along the waterfront the great peninsula which reaches to the Lizard was as if it had never been; even the Mount was no more than a shadow. Sea and sky and land were merged in a moist grey continuum and though it was not actually raining the screen wipers were in constant use. April had once more changed her mood.

They turned off the main road out of the town towards St. Hilary. Kersey said: "You don't seem very upset, sir."

"At least it gives me an excuse for doing what I intended to do anyway."

The fire tender and a police patrol car were parked close to the stile where the footpath through the scrub left the road. They were pumping water from a nearby stream and a hose snaked over the stile and up through the undergrowth. The fire was almost out but smoke and steam rose like the Israelites' pillar of cloud in the moist, still air, and everywhere there was the acrid smell of charred wood.

The fire officer said: "It went up like tinder; we might as well not have come for all the good we could do."

"Deliberate, presumably?"

"It certainly looks that way but we shall know better when we've had a chance to examine the debris. I gather you've got an interest here apart from possible arson?"

"You could say that."

Wycliffe and Kersey crossed the stile and followed the path up through the gorse to the site of the little hut. There were two uniformed men from the local nick and a couple of firemen. In the capricious way of fires, much of the back wall of the hut and the frame of one end still stood; the roof had vanished and the floor had collapsed into the cavity below it; the verandah steps were intact and the planks of the verandah itself, though heavily charred, were still in place. In the cavity below where the floor had been Wycliffe could see the carbonized framework of the settee lying at a drunken angle.

One of the uniformed men said: "PC Evans, sir. We observed the fire from the road at 0450 and, after investigation, alerted the brigade. The place was well alight and unapproachable; there seemed a risk that the fire might extend to the scrub."

"All right; you couldn't do anything, you reported on your radio and asked for assistance. Did anyone turn up from the house?"

"Not at once, sir. The brigade arrived at 0510; Glynn and his son showed up a little later. Glynn said he happened to wake and saw the glow through his window."

"What was his attitude?"

Evans hesitated. "Well, puzzled is the best word I can think of. He really didn't seem to know what to make of it."

"Where are they now?"

"I insisted that they go back to the house, sir."

"All right; you can get back now and put in your report." Wycliffe turned to Kersey: "Get Fox over here; he was expecting to come anyway after the briefing. You'd better stay. As soon as it's at all practicable I want the debris cleared from the cavity under the hut floor."

"Shouldn't we get Forensic in on it?"

"To hell with Forensic! Fox is quite capable of handling this. I'm going up to the house and I shall be there if you want me."

The front door stood open to the slate-flagged passage. He looked in the one-time dining-room but it was empty. Through the open front door a damp chill seemed to have invaded and taken possession of the whole house. Wycliffe heard voices somewhere at the back and he went down the passage, past the stairs. The voices came from the kitchen. Through the half-open door he could see a sink and draining-board with a wooden plate-rack over.

A woman's voice was saying: "I told him nothing, Maurice, but if I'm asked direct questions I don't intend to lie." She broke off. "What's the matter with you, for God's sake? You're shivering! Let me make you a cup of coffee or something . . . Where's David?"

"I don't know; he was here not long before you came."

Wycliffe tapped on the door and pushed it open. Molly Pearce was in the act of running water into an electric kettle while Maurice stood, hands thrust deep into his trouser pockets, looking utterly dejected.

Molly was the first to recover her poise: "I came down to see if I could be of any use."

Wycliffe said: "I'm quite sure you will be, Miss Pearce."

Maurice had momentary difficulty in finding his voice. "I don't know what to say about this fire, Mr. Wycliffe."

"It will be time enough to talk about that when we have completed our investigation. Now there are other more important things." His manner was brusque, but not unfriendly.

Maurice looked uneasily at Molly Pearce. "Perhaps we should go into the other room. Molly won't want—"

"We can talk well enough here and I would rather Miss Pearce stayed." Wycliffe turned to the woman: "Go on with the coffee if you want to; I'm sure Mr. Glynn can do with it."

The kitchen could not have changed significantly since the Glynn family shifted *en bloc* into town nearly thirty years earlier. And it was still essentially a farmhouse kitchen as it had been for long before that. The floor was of stone slabs covered with matting; the massive farmhouse table was still there though the top was covered with heat-resisting plastic. The walls were painted a dreary green and ranged against them were an electric cooker, a refrigerator, and a washing-machine. The Glynns moved with reluctance into the modern world.

Wycliffe was in no hurry; he ambled about the room with apparent aimlessness and Maurice watched him as a cat watches the restless peregrinations of a strange dog. Molly Pearce went on preparing the coffee but she hardly took her eyes off him.

Then, at a certain point, Wycliffe said: "Why don't you sit down, Mr. Glynn? After all, it's your house."

He spoke casually but Maurice pulled up a kitchen stool, sat on it, and seemed to relax.

Good policemen are actors, they acquire a persona which is both authoritarian and inquisitorial without, by nature, being either. Over the years Wycliffe had developed a technique of interview which blended the man with the persona and seemed to achieve results.

Molly put three mugs on the table. "Milk for you, Mr. Wycliffe?"

"No thanks."

Maurice sat on his stool, his long legs twined around its legs. He was unshaven, his eyes seemed sunken and dark in contrast with his pallid skin.

"I want to ask you both one or two questions about things that happened a long time ago, but before I start I'll tell you what I know already so that we have no misunderstanding."

He turned to face Maurice Glynn and his manner was conversational: "I know that at the time of your wife's illness you were

having an affair with your sister-in-law, Inez. You met when you
could on Sundays in the little hut; one of her woman friends acted
as a go-between, passing messages, in particular letting Inez know
whether your wife would be spending the weekend at home or in
hospital. Either out of caution or from a sense of propriety the
two of you did not meet if your wife was at home."

Maurice said: "I really can't see what that has to do with what
has happened recently."

There was an old wall clock over the mantelpiece which struck
the hour on a coiled wire and it chose this moment to dole out
eight tinny strokes. Wycliffe waited until it was over then went on
as though Maurice had not spoken.

"You may not know it, but Matthew was kept informed of these
meetings through a number of anonymous letters." He paused,
looking first at Maurice, then at Molly Pearce.

Molly returned his gaze in silence, apparently unperturbed.
Maurice seemed about to speak but changed his mind.

"Now for my questions: Sunday 20th March 1971—a long time
ago, but I'm sure you both remember it; it was the day Inez was
seen by her family for the last time. Was your wife at home or in
hospital on that day, Mr. Glynn?"

"She was at home." Maurice was holding his coffee mug half-
way to his lips but he did not drink.

"Had you sent the usual message through your go-between,
warning Inez not to come?"

Maurice hesitated for some time before saying: "Yes."

Wycliffe seemed in no hurry; there were long intervals between
question and answer accentuated by the silence; it was as though
time itself had become sluggish.

"So why did she come?"

"She didn't come."

"You didn't see Inez that Sunday?"

"No, I did not see her."

Wycliffe turned to Molly Pearce. "And yet Matthew received an
anonymous note saying that Inez's car was in Badgers' Wood on
that day."

Again Molly said nothing but this time Wycliffe persisted: "Miss
Pearce, I'm going to ask you an important question and I would

like an answer: did you see Inez's Mini parked in the pine wood that Sunday?"

She looked at Maurice before saying: "Yes, I did."

"Mr. Glynn?"

Maurice put down his mug and spoke in a low voice. "If Inez came that day I didn't see her. We had an arrangement in case of any slip-up: she would wait for me in the hut and if I didn't come she would go again."

"When did your wife return to hospital?"

"On Sunday evening; a weekend at home meant that I fetched her on Friday and took her back on Sunday evening."

"I see." Wycliffe stood up. "Well, that is all for the present. Later you may be asked to make statements about what precisely happened during that weekend."

They had assumed that his questions were only beginning and he was at the door before either of them realized that it was over. Maurice followed him down the passage. On the doorstep he said: "I don't understand what's happening, Mr. Wycliffe."

Wycliffe said nothing and walked on down the drive.

Through the open door of the workshop he could see Chris and David in close embrace. Although the boy was a head taller she was patting his shoulder as one consoles a child.

Wycliffe muttered to himself: "Babes in the Wood is about it!"

It was afternoon and the debris of the hut had cooled off sufficiently to be handled. Fox and his two assistants began the work of clearing the brick-walled cavity below where the floor of the hut had been. Each partially carbonized beam or strut or plank was lifted out and laid on the grass of the clearing. Those contents of the hut which had survived the fire were similarly treated: the paraffin stove, badly buckled, with every scrap of paint burned off; the framework of the settee, which fell to pieces as soon as an attempt was made to shift it; a chair, badly charred, but intact; a metal cupboard; a galvanized bucket; a stool . . .

When they had cleared the larger items, there remained, apart from a mass of burnt paper, half-consumed books, and charred fabric, a multitude of smaller things, from items of cutlery and cups and saucers to a much damaged pair of binoculars and a radio. Fox gave as much attention to each find as an archaeologist devotes to his artefacts. At intervals he stopped the work to record progress on film. When most of the debris had been cleared they had reached the more or less level surface of an earth floor.

Wycliffe and Kersey, resplendent in yellow oilskins, stood by. The mist had not lifted, the grass was sodden, and globules of moisture glistened on every spine of gorse. A female blackbird went on with the serious business of provisioning her brood somewhere close at hand, ignoring the disturbance.

Kersey said: "No sign of how the fire was started."

Wycliffe was morose. "Somebody broke in, splashed paraffin over the place and set it alight or, perhaps, he set up a delayed-action incendiary device with a bucket of paraffin and a lighted candle floated on top. I don't know and I don't damn well care how it started or which idiot started it!"

Kersey said: "Sorry I spoke."

Now Fox and his helpers were retrieving quite small objects from the floor of the cavity; scratching around in the soil which was calcined in parts, untouched by the heat in others. They turned up some coins, an old fountain-pen, glass bottles and jars, nails, screws . . . Fox garnered them all into his harvest.

Finally he looked up at Wycliffe: "I think that's it, sir."

Wycliffe said: "The soil level is a good deal higher in the cavity than the ground outside—try a probe."

Fox looked stubborn. "You wouldn't expect a concrete base in a building of this sort, sir."

"I'm not looking for a concrete base."

Fox pressed a stick down into the soil and it sank easily. He tried in a number of places with the same result.

"Try nearer the front of the hut."

At the second try the probe met resistance at a depth of about a foot and successive probes met similar resistance in a line close to and parallel with the front of the hut.

Wycliffe said: "This is where you start digging."

There was no problem; within the boundaries of the brick foundations the ground was soft and unconsolidated. Fox and one of his assistants worked with care and within a very short time they had uncovered parts of what seemed to be a roll of black polythene. A few minutes more and it was clear that what they had found was something that had been rolled in polythene and made up into a rough parcel, the shape and size of which resembled a human mummy.

"Photographs, Fox."

Kersey said: "So you've found what you were looking for, sir, a gilt-edged motive all neatly wrapped up."

Wycliffe was too preoccupied to take the bait. "Get hold of Dr. Rees and ask him to come here; then locate Franks and try to have a word with him. Explain to Rees and to him what's going on."

"Am I supposed to know?"

Wycliffe snapped: "Don't be childish! By the way, Rees had better come prepared—and we shall need the van."

Dr. Rees looked down into the pit. "What have you got there, for God's sake?"

"That's what I want you to tell me."

With the aid of plastic slings they hoisted the bundle out of the pit and on to a sheet spread on the ground. It had been tied about in several places with nylon cord which, like the polythene, showed little sign of deterioration.

Wycliffe said: "Expose just enough for us to be sure of what we've got."

Wearing surgical gloves and a mask Rees slit a nylon cord at what appeared to be the head end. The polythene had been doubled over at the ends and had to be folded back and spread out.

Rees said: "How long is it?"

"Seventeen years if I'm right."

"So we can expect anything. Interesting to see what effect bundling up a corpse in polythene may have—whether mummification or the formation of adipocere takes over."

He parted the edges of the polythene and spread it abroad revealing a human head. The most striking feature was the rich black hair which seemed to have changed little from its condition in life. The face was repulsive, mainly because the eye sockets appeared to be empty and something had happened to the end of the nose and the lips, exposing the teeth. Even so Wycliffe believed that anyone who had known that face in life would recognize it now.

"Cover her up."

Rees said: "Inez."

"You knew her?"

"As a patient."

Wycliffe turned to the men with a stretcher. "Take her away."

When they were gone Kersey said: "You want me to bring him in?"

"Maurice?"

"Who else?"

"When we bring him in I want to be in a position to hold him."

"But we could charge him, for God's sake!"

Wycliffe's manner relaxed. "We are getting at cross-purposes, Doug. You assume that Maurice killed his brother Matthew because Matthew intended to build houses on this site, a scheme which would have been sure to uncover what we have just found."

"Yes; evidence of his earlier crime. And you don't agree with that?"

"The point is that unless Sara changes her testimony it would be futile to charge Maurice with the murder of his brother; we could never make it stick."

"Perhaps not but there's enough circumstantial evidence to charge him with the murder of his brother's wife."

Wycliffe hesitated. "Bring him in for questioning in connection with the discovery of Inez Glynn's body. We can probably find a holding charge there if we need it. Agreed?"

Kersey was mollified. "You're the boss."

Wycliffe said: "I'll join you at the nick as soon as I can."

The white light shone down on the outstretched form which was clothed as a woman: a blue, woollen jumper and a quality tweed skirt. Pinned to the jumper at the breast was a silver brooch in the shape of a butterfly.

Something unspeakable had happened to the legs, and the shoes—walking shoes for the discerning countrywoman—were splayed at an angle unattainable in life. The neck, impossibly shrivelled, was hung about with a double string of white coral beads. Then there was the face, the head, and the hair . . .

Wycliffe said: "Thank God you no longer use formalin."

Franks contemplated his subject. "She'll go into the textbooks. In view of the type of soil, preservation is quite remarkable. I've tidied her up as much as I can; who's going to identify her?"

"The sister-in-law, Sara Glynn—she's on her way with Lucy Lane."

"Good! Then I'll be able to get on."

Franks and his assistant covered the body with a sheet and they all moved into the anteroom where an attendant sat at a desk.

Wycliffe said: "The clothes will go to Forensic though I don't imagine they will tell us much. Any ideas yet about how she died?"

"Off the record: she was hit on the head, then throttled. Your killer seems to have a one-track mind."

They waited, but not for long: the wall clock in the dismal little room showed ten minutes to six when Sara came in followed by Lucy Lane. She was desperately pale but she had herself well under control. She glanced about the room, acknowledged Wycliffe, hesitated, then in a low voice she said: "I must talk to you. May I come to the Incident Room this evening?"

"It will have to be late, I'm unlikely to be there before nine."

"I'll come at nine and wait." She turned to the white-coated Franks; Lucy Lane followed them into the next room. They were gone very briefly. When Sara returned she looked shaken. Lucy piloted her to the desk. The attendant murmured: "Do you positively identify the body you have just seen as that of your sister-in-law, Inez Glynn?"

"Yes."

"Then perhaps you will sign here."

Sara signed.

Wycliffe was back in his little office, initialling reports. The church clock chimed and struck seven. The mist which had persisted through the day was denser than ever and the view from his window was limited to the neighbouring slate roofs gleaming with moisture. Now and then he could hear the bleat of a distant foghorn. There was a tap at the door and Lucy Lane came in.

"Molly Pearce is here, sir."

"Ask her to come in."

Molly wore a thin woollen frock, apple green, with a matching cardigan. She looked composed. Wycliffe placed a chair.

"I've asked you to come here because the situation has changed since this morning. You know that, I suppose?"

"Yes."

"The body found under the burned-out hut was Inez Glynn's and the pathologist says that she was murdered. You are here voluntarily and you are free to go whenever you wish. On the other hand I think you can help us by answering one or two questions."

"I understand."

"It was you who wrote those anonymous notes to Matthew Glynn telling him of his wife's infidelity?"

"Yes." She looked away. "I could say that I did it out of sympathy for Celia—Maurice's wife. I wish that were true."

"Your conduct only concerns me in so far as it may help to explain what happened on the day Inez Glynn disappeared. You told me this morning that you saw Inez's car in the pine wood that Sunday. At what time did you see it?"

"I saw it first at about eleven in the morning and again late in the afternoon. I was puzzled to find it there on a day when Celia was supposed to be home."

"Did you call at Trebyan during that time?"

She flushed. "Actually I was there twice, once in the morning and again at about five. The second time it was to give Celia some eggs to take back with her—we had hens in those days. They were just leaving when I arrived—Maurice was taking her back to the hospital."

She added after a pause: "There was nothing unusual about me calling to see Celia; we got on well before she was ill and whenever she was home I would look in at least once. It seemed to cheer her up."

"As far as you could tell, was everything as usual with Maurice and between Maurice and his wife?"

"Yes; actually Celia seemed a lot better than the last time I'd seen her. She even asked about David which was quite new; usually just to mention the boy's name was enough to upset her. That was why he always went to stay with his Aunt Sara when his mother was home."

It was almost eight when Wycliffe arrived at the police station to join Kersey.

"He's in the interview room; he's been offered a meal but settled for coffee."

Maurice Glynn was seated at a bare table in a little room with a high window. There was a tape recorder on a shelf near the empty chair on the other side of the table. A uniformed man stood just inside the door and a framed notice on one wall advised the subject of his legal rights. Maurice wore the jeans and denim jacket in which Wycliffe had always seen him. He looked ineffably weary.

Kersey took his seat; Wycliffe remained standing. Kersey switched on the tape recorder and, very brisk, recited the formalities, ending with the caution: "You do not have to say anything but what you do say may be taken down and used in evidence. This interview begins at 2008 hours.

"You recall Sunday 20th March 1971?"

"Yes."

"Your wife was home from hospital for the weekend and your infant son was staying with his aunt in Penzance; is that correct?"

"Yes."

"You were not expecting a visit from your sister-in-law, Inez?"

"No."

"Why not?"

"Because I had sent a message to say my wife would be home."

"Did you know that throughout the day her car was parked in the pine wood adjoining Roskear Farm?"

"I did not know it at the time."

"When did you discover that it was in fact parked there?"

The first moment of hesitation, then: "Molly—Miss Pearce—mentioned it to me on the quiet."

Wycliffe intervened. "Molly Pearce visited you twice on that day; on which visit did she mention the car?"

"The second; she came just as I was about to drive my wife back to the hospital."

"What did you do?"

"I did nothing then. I was very puzzled and worried. When I returned from taking my wife back I went to the pine wood to see for myself, and Inez's car was still there. I couldn't understand it."

Maurice had started calmly; now he was becoming agitated; he began to move uneasily in his chair and he kept clasping and unclasping his hands which were resting on the table in front of him.

"Once more: what did you do?"

"It was getting dark by this time but I decided to look in the hut to see if she had left any message. I just couldn't think of any explanation . . ."

"Go on."

"I went down to the hut; the door was shut and everything seemed normal. I opened the door . . . And then I saw her. She was lying on the settee; her skirt was pulled up and her knickers were around her ankles; it looked as though she had been raped . . . And then I saw her face . . . There was a wire twisted around her neck . . . She was dead."

He looked so pale that Wycliffe thought he might faint. "Would you like a glass of water?"

Maurice shook his head. "I didn't kill her! I didn't! My God, why should I ever want to? She was keeping me sane; I mean, with my wife in hospital and the child and the pottery . . ."

He was trembling.

"So what did you do?"

"I don't know what I did. I couldn't think. Then I realized that I must phone the police . . . I went back to the house and I had the telephone in my hand when I suddenly saw the position I was in; a man having an affair with his brother's wife while his own wife was mentally ill . . . The woman strangled on the settee where . . ." His voice failed him and it was a moment or two before he could go on. He made a vague gesture. "It seemed impossible that I would be believed . . . I mean, how could it have been anybody else?" He looked from Kersey to Wycliffe, a wild look. "I reached such a point that I half believed I'd done it!"

There was a long pause then he went on more quietly: "It would have killed my wife . . ." He put his hands over his eyes. "I've lived for seventeen years with the nightmare which started then . . .''

"What did you do?"

"I realized that I must get rid of the body—hide it. There were loose floorboards in the hut. I got some of the black polythene we use for warming the soil for early crops and I wrapped her in it and tied it around her as tightly as I could, then I removed the boards and lowered her body into the space under the floor."

"When did you do this?"

"I don't know; I'd lost count of time but it must have been early in the night. I know I had the lamps lit in the hut."

"Go on."

"I had to get rid of the car. I thought of driving it into a quarry or over a cliff . . . But I knew it would be found. Then I thought of making it look as though she'd gone away—I decided to drive the car to some place where she might have arranged to meet somebody, and Exeter seemed the sort of place . . . I was desperate . . ."

"Did you take any precautions to avoid leaving traces in the car?"

"I wore gloves."

"How did you get back?"

"I parked the car in the station car-park and caught the early-morning train. I didn't go all the way to Penzance where they know me at the station, I got off at St. Erth and walked; it's only four miles . . ."

Wycliffe said: "When the body was found it was buried in the earth."

He nodded. "Over the next few days—weeks, I don't know!—I dug a trench and laid her in it, then I heaped on soil that I wheeled down in a barrow and I levelled it off. After that I nailed the floorboards down . . ."

He leaned back in his chair and looked at them with a curiously blank stare. "Nothing happened . . . Nothing happened! Nobody asked me a single question!" His voice was rising hysterically; once more he covered his face with his hands and this time he burst into tears.

Kersey's calm voice dictated to the tape: "This interview interrupted at 2031 hours."

Wycliffe left Kersey at the police station and walked back to the town centre. It was almost dark and the town was quiet. His mind was in turmoil. Almost thirty years ago Alfred Glynn had planned to marry Inez and started a chain of events which twelve years later had led to murder and, seventeen years after that, to a second murder and a suicide. Perhaps the strangest aspect of the affair was that during those twenty-nine years the family had been able to present a public image of normal, perhaps above-average respectability.

With something approaching desperation Wycliffe was trying to see the events in perspective, to relate them one to another and to imagine the repressed tensions and the accumulating bitterness which had finally surfaced. But what troubled him most was the thought that he was being pushed beyond his role as an investigating officer into decisions which were either moral or judicial or both.

He turned down into Lady Street and was greeted by a southerly breeze which stirred the moisture-laden air and promised a clearer night. He passed a restaurant where the tables were visible from the street and was reminded that he had not eaten, but he was in no mood for food. At the Incident Room the duty officer said: "Sara Glynn is here, sir; she says you are expecting her."

Sara was in the smallest of the three rooms, seated on a hard kitchen chair, her legs tucked in, her handbag and gloves in her lap. She wore a dark green raincoat.

"I'm sorry if I've kept you waiting."

"It doesn't matter."

He took her into his office and settled her in a chair by his desk. "You have something to tell me?"

It was clear that she was having difficulty in choosing her words though he had no doubt that she had rehearsed the occasion. Finally she spoke: "There is something I want to make clear— something which, if it is not understood between us, could create unnecessary difficulty and suffering."

He waited.

"I want you to understand that I did see Alfred leaving by the yard door when I returned from my walk last Saturday evening." She spoke slowly, emphasizing every word. "He was distraught— so far gone that I doubt if he even saw me though I tried to speak to him." She paused for a moment or two as though to lend further weight to her words. "I suspect that you do not believe me —that is up to you, but it is the evidence I shall give wherever and whenever I am required to testify."

"In other words you stand by your statement."

"I do, and I shall."

"Perhaps you had some additional reason for coming here?" He was polite but distant.

"There was something else. I would like you to know that my brother Matthew was not a man to turn the other cheek. It was a very great surprise to me that he seemed to accept his wife's infidelity; a very great surprise."

It was as though she was teaching a lesson to a child, speaking slowly and distinctly, and offering one simple idea at a time.

"When did you last speak to your brother Maurice?"

"I was with him this afternoon when the police came to take him away."

The pride in her voice was unmistakable.

She got up from her chair, gathering together her handbag and gloves. "That is what I came to say, Mr. Wycliffe."

Wycliffe saw her off the premises and watched her as she walked up the steep alley and disappeared into the darkness. A remarkable woman.

CHAPTER TWELVE

Friday morning

Wycliffe had spent an hour at divisional headquarters for a media briefing and he was depressed; the reporters believed that he was holding out on them whereas he only wished that he had something to hold out about.

"The body has been identified as that of Mrs. Inez Glynn who went missing from her home on March 20th 1971."

"And she'd been there ever since?"

"That seems likely."

"How was she killed?"

"The indications are that she had been strangled."

"So you are now looking for the killer of Matthew Glynn and his wife?"

"We are investigating two homicides."

"Two killers or one?"

"That remains to be seen."

"Maurice Glynn is still in custody?"

"Mr. Glynn is providing us with information which may be useful to our inquiry."

"Are you expecting to bring charges in the near future?"

"We haven't made an arrest yet."

That was the substance but the questions and the answers were repeated in various disguises *ad nauseam.*

A tap at the door and Kersey came in carrying a tape recorder and looking dynamic. "Good morning, sir! Maurice's statement—second instalment." He put the little machine on the table and ran the tape to the position of his choice. "Listen to this!"

Kersey's voice on the tape: "Who did you think had killed her? You must have thought about it."

A longish pause, then Maurice, speaking in a low voice: "Oh, yes, I thought about it . . . It seems I thought about nothing else for God knows how long . . . I couldn't sleep, I was on tranquillizers . . ."

"You haven't answered the question."

"No; I haven't answered the question. Sometimes I thought it must have been Matthew; sometimes Alfred . . . sometimes that it could only have been some pervert, a stranger . . . Then I remembered that Inez shouldn't have been there if our arrangements had worked . . ."

"And?"

"I wondered if she'd arranged to meet somebody else there; it wouldn't have surprised me. More than half her kicks came from taking pointless risks."

"But she left her car in the wood—the chances were you would find out."

The tape ran in silence for several seconds then Maurice said in a voice that sounded desperately weary: "You think that would have bothered her?"

"So in seventeen years you reached no conclusion?"

"Does that surprise you?" He sounded frustrated; perhaps by his questioner's lack of understanding. "I didn't even want to. Mainly I wanted to forget, and in recent years I've come damn near succeeding."

The telephone cut across the growing tension. Wycliffe picked up the instrument, snapped: "No calls!" and slammed it down.

Kersey's tape voice was saying: "What started it up again?"

"Isn't it obvious? Matthew's houses started it up again." There was a tremor in the voice on the tape. "To me it seemed like Nemesis . . ."

Another long pause which Kersey did not interrupt, then Maurice went on: "It was only when I went to see Matthew, when we had that row, that I realized it was all a trap."

"A trap?"

"Don't you see? He knew what he was doing to me and after Mother's death there was nothing to stop him . . . He must have gloated over it for years . . . He didn't have to build the houses, only threaten . . . If I was scared of being accused when it happened, where would I be now?" The sentence ended in a dry sob.

"Did you or he refer to his wife's death?"

"Not a word! I didn't dare and he didn't need to. I can't describe his attitude—challenging and at the same time, contemptuous. My God, I understood!"

The tape was silent for so long that Wycliffe thought it was over then Kersey's voice came, softly insinuating: "So you killed him."

There was a quick intake of breath then, speaking through his teeth, with hysterical emphasis: "I did not kill him! He deserved to die, but I did not kill him!"

Kersey switched off the tape and they were silent for a while; then Wycliffe said: "And Sara will back him up to the last ditch." He lifted his arms and let them fall to his sides in a gesture of helplessness. "Now we are in the trap."

Wycliffe spent the next half-hour on the telephone to Bertram Oldroyd, the chief constable.

Oldroyd summed up: "So in your view, Charles, there are no grounds for believing that Maurice Glynn was responsible for the woman's death?"

"None. Apart from the absence of any apparent motive he doesn't seem to have had the opportunity either; it wasn't until late evening on that Sunday that he knew she was there. Fox is carrying on at the scene but I don't expect much; I haven't had Franks's final report but he isn't hopeful of being able to tell us anything beyond the cause of death."

"Then it's down to Matthew."

"Yes, and Matthew is dead so there is nothing we can do about that."

"But Matthew's own death? The sister says she saw Alfred coming away from the scene that night. Do we accept that?"

Wycliffe was dour. "Sara is the sole witness; she made a statement to that effect and she will stick to it come hell or high water. As to my believing her, that's another matter."

Oldroyd spoke softly: "What *do* you believe, Charles?"

Wycliffe sighed with weariness. "I believe that Sara is a determined and clever woman; I believe that it was Maurice she saw, not Alfred; I believe that she went to work on Alfred, destroying his illusions and with them his reason for living.

"Alfred killed himself, but even if he had lived he was so disorientated that his testimony would have been worthless."

"So we are left with framing charges against Maurice: concealing a death and the unlawful disposal of a corpse. From then on it's up to the coroner. If his verdict names names that's up to him. You agree?"

"I have to."

"Good! I want you back, Charles. We shan't come out of this with much kudos but at least the lawyers won't make their fortunes."

The professional view.

Wycliffe believed the criminal law should aim at damage limitation rather than at some abstraction called justice. With a profound sense of irony he now asked himself whether Sara had carried his argument to its logical conclusion. God knows enough people were going to suffer, in particular the innocent, and who would benefit from Maurice Glynn spending fifteen years in a squalid jail?

But such relativism troubled his conscience which was still the property of his Methodist upbringing. He was also troubled professionally, because he had failed.

He sent for Lucy Lane and made her listen to the tapes of Maurice's interviews, then he told her of his conversation with the chief constable.

"This is a damnable case, Lucy. I want you to talk to the family; explain the meaning of the charges against Maurice; the significance of the adjourned inquests on Matthew and on Alfred; and of the inquest which will now be held on Inez. They must understand too that although no charges can be brought against the dead there is nothing to stop the coroner naming them in his verdicts. I doubt if he will but they should be prepared. You understand?"

Lucy Lane knew her Wycliffe. "I think so, sir. You want me to put them out of their misery as far as the facts allow without fouling any of the legal trip-wires."

Wycliffe's smile was thin. "You should have been a lawyer, Lucy."

Wycliffe drove himself to Trebyan that afternoon; he went alone because it was a private thing. For the first time that day he noticed that the sun was shining. The white gate was open and he swept up the drive past the tethered goats and into the same stillness he had known on his first visit, but this time he could not bring himself to shatter it by ringing the brass bell. The front door was open to the stone-flagged hall but he did not go in.

He found them in the workshop unloading the kiln, and stood in the doorway as they dismantled the edifice of biscuit-fired pots and pitchers, bowls and beakers, transferring them to wooden shelves. When they saw him they stopped as though transfixed.

"I want to talk to you."

They seemed to move with unnatural slowness. It was Christine who said: "Do you want to go into the house?"

"That would be best."

In the former dining-room it was Christine who offered Wycliffe a chair, then she and the boy sat side by side on the sofa. David spoke first but Wycliffe felt sure he had been prompted.

"My father didn't set fire to the hut, I did."

Wycliffe was dismissive. "An idiotic thing to do. You thought you were protecting your father against something with no idea what. In fact we found what we expected to find so what you did is no concern of mine; it's between you and your father."

Christine reached out her hand and placed it on the boy's knee. David's face had been pale, now it was flushed.

Wycliffe went on: "Miss Lane must have explained the situation to you. All I can say is that your father is being released on police bail this afternoon."

They sat motionless, afraid to ask questions; afraid almost to breathe. In the end it was Christine who spoke. "What sort of sentence is Uncle Maurice likely to get?"

"I can't predict what the court will do but whatever the sen-

tence a large part of it—perhaps all of it—is likely to be suspended."

Christine went on in a voice that was barely recognizable: "And
about my father?"

"The police accept your aunt's statement. No action can be
taken against a dead man so, after the inquest, the case will be
closed."

Christine's fingers tightened over the boy's knee and he placed
his hand over hers.

Wycliffe said: "This is a terrible time for you both; you must
make up your minds to see it through."

Christine nodded. "We shall go on as before—as nearly as they
will let us."

On the night before the funeral Gina, Gerald and Barry were in
the kitchen, seated around the table, picking away at cold food.

Gina said: "God, I wish tomorrow was over!"

Her husband tried to be consoling. "It will be a purely family
thing; nobody has been asked to come; we haven't even made an
announcement."

Gerald spoke with his mouth full. "The press will be there; you
won't keep them out."

Gina stood up. "I'll make the coffee."

Sara was in her bedroom, standing in front of her wardrobe mirror. She wore a charcoal-grey coat with a fur collar which she had
discarded four or five years ago. She turned this way and that in a
critical inspection of her image in the glass.

"It still fits . . . I suppose it will do."

About the Author

W. J. Burley is the author of many novels of mystery and suspense, including *Wycliffe and the Tangled Web* and *Wycliffe and the Winsor Blue*, both published by the Crime Club. He is a graduate of Oxford with a degree in zoology, and he makes his home in Cornwall, England.